THE DOOMSDAY VAULT

THE SCIENCE OFFICER: VOLUME 5

BLAZE WARD

KNOTTED ROAD PRESS

The Doomsday Vault
Volume 5
Blaze Ward
Copyright © 2017 Blaze Ward
All rights reserved
Published by Knotted Road Press
www.KnottedRoadPress.com

ISBN: 978-1-943663-47-7

Cover art:
Copyright © Philcold | Dreamstime.com - Alien Space Base Photo

Cover and interior design copyright © 2017 Knotted Road Press

Never miss a release!
If you'd like to be notified of new releases, sign up for my newsletter.

I only send out newsletters once a quarter, will never spam you, or use your email for nefarious purposes. You can also unsubscribe at any time.

http://www.blazeward.com/newsletter/

Greater Than The Gods Intended

Other Science Fiction Stories

Myrmirdons

Moonshot

Menelaus

Earthquake Gun

Moscow Gold

Fairchild

White Crane

***The Collective* Universe**

The Shipwrecked Mermaid

Imposters

BOOK THIRTEEN: CALYPSO

PART ONE

JAVIER ARITZA GLANCED up from the complicated electronic board that made up his duty station as Science Officer aboard the private-service, semi-piratical, Strike Corvette *Storm Gauntlet*. The bridge around him was quiet but poised. The walls were kinda gray today, but the crew wasn't.

Leaning forward, as his mother would have said.

Angry sharks smelling blood, as his first captain, back in the *Concord* fleet days, might have phrased it.

Javier turned his head far enough to make eye contact with Captain Zakhar Sokolov, seated atop his command throne chair at the rear of the chamber, everyone else in front of him where he could track them like an omniscient being.

"I don't want to hear it, Javier," the man growled. It would have been under his breath, but everyone on the bridge probably heard it in the empty stillness. "In fact, if you say it again, I'm going to start a curse kitty and charge you a quarter drachma every time you mutter it. We'll use that to fund orphanages, or something."

Even seated on his command chair, like a king atop a

throne, it would be easy to mistake the captain for merely average. There wasn't much that made Zakhar Sokolov stand out. Mid-fifties. Typical Anglo skin color. Shaved head. Salt and pepper Van Dyke. Average height. Average build.

Javier grinned at the thought. Then he dug into a pocket for a coin and flipped it noisily into the air with his thumb in the captain's direction.

"This does not feel right," Javier announced, having paid good money for the privilege. "I realize we're only expecting to ambush a broken-down, half-blind freighter, but my recommendation would be to go in fully silent, and use extraordinary measures, since you don't want to leave."

Give the man credit. Javier got to watch Sokolov count to ten before he sighed quietly. And he pocketed the coin.

"Based on?" Sokolov asked in a voice used to dealing with an annoying, rambunctious eight-year-old in the backseat.

"While you've been watching for the big, bad wolf, I've been scanning the planet below us," Javier retorted, trying to not sound too smug about things.

You know, just slightly smug, without totally overdoing it.

The ship's dragoon, Djamila Sykora, gave him a good dose of stinkeye from her station across the bridge, but nothing she had going today was going to dent his mood. Not even a 2.1 meter tall, killer-Amazon, bad-ass, close-combat specialist known as the *Ballerina of Death*.

Sokolov didn't even speak, just posed a question with his face. A sad, put-upon, dad-face.

"The place was terraformed," Javier continued. "But it was done early on, during the Resource Wars era. And it didn't work. Life never really took, and it will probably revert to being a dead rock in another hundred thousand years or so."

"And?" Zakhar cast the word into the space between Javier's thoughts.

"There is nobody down there," Javier replied. "No lights. No radio signals. Nothing. And any time you spend on the surface you should have supplemental oxygen handy, as well as a warmsuit, because it is comparable to living at three-thousand-meters elevation, barely above freezing water, in the best places. The farther you get away from the equator, the worse it gets."

"Somebody is paying us good money to hijack a cargo," Zakhar observed.

Sokolov turned on that captain's charisma thing Javier had never managed for more than five minutes at a time.

He was *The Captain*, all of a sudden.

Javier nodded, an evil grin forming on his face.

"Those people are not delivering that cargo to anyone on *Svalbard*," Javier replied.

A beam of electricity seemed to connect the men, the only two here that had been trained, once upon a time, at the *Concord* Academy at *Bryce*.

"They're meeting someone," Zakhar said, mostly to himself. "And nobody mentioned that to me."

Javier just nodded.

"Alert Status One," Sokolov ordered in a hard voice. "Engage full stealth mode. Now."

Suddenly, the bridge sounded like a *Concord* warship going into harm's way instead of a civilian pirate sneaking around.

Javier flipped a single switch on his board that shut everything down to passive scans only.

He might have been sand-bagging the old man. After all, *Storm Gauntlet* had stolen all the sensor packages from Javier's old probe-cutter *Mielikki*. Right now, even on passive, his scan capabilities were probably better than most front-line warships in active mode, let alone freighters.

He had already mapped one hundred and fifty-three minor moons and major asteroids moving around in the darkness between planets.

"Nav," Sokolov continued. "Find me a different orbital path immediately. Your choice. Not here."

The pilot, Piet Alferdinck, nodded and began to play a complicated piano concerto on the board in front of him.

Javier repressed a sigh. His old ship, *Mielikki*, had been piloted by a full AI package, a *Sentience* named Suvi. In fact, Javier had been the whole crew.

Well, him and four chickens.

He missed that.

One of these days, he was going to see a great many of the people around him hung from a high yardarm in low gravity for cutting Suvi's ship, her corpse, apart. He had only barely managed to smuggle her personality chips out in a bucket of chicken feed and then pour her into his sensor remote, a planet-side surveying tool about the size of a large grapefruit.

There were days that young lady liked to remind him how much greater she used to be. But she had to do it quietly. If the pirates found out about her, they'd probably execute him in a heartbeat, regardless of the number of times he had saved their asses.

What they did to her after that wouldn't be worth mentioning.

"Stealth mode engaged, Captain," a voice called.

Deep. Male. Surprisingly smooth. Kibwe Bousaid, the captain's executive assistant and general do-it-all.

"Stay alert, but stand down to a small crew footprint under the science officer until we have incoming signals," the captain called, rising from his station. "I'll be in my office."

He took two steps and then pivoted to face Javier.

"We were hired to do a job, mister," Zakhar intoned seriously.

Javier nodded once, just as serious. He might act like a goofball most of the time, but there was absolutely no margin for error when the trap you had set might suddenly turn inside out on you.

PART TWO

Javier kinda enjoyed being in command, as long as he didn't have to actually do anything captainy.

About half the bridge crew had departed with the captain. Paperwork, certifications, stuff.

The dragoon, Sykora, had stayed put, but she was busy knitting. He would have guessed it was a sweater for herself, if pressed. She had laid out one whole back piece like the tanned hide of her latest victim. It didn't help his state of mind that she was working in a dark, almost umber-colored, yarn, about the color of his skin if he didn't get enough tan.

She probably knew that.

As long as she and her cannibal tendencies stayed on that side of the bridge, he'd be fine. They'd all be fine.

A chirp brought Javier back to the present.

Somebody had dropped out of jump a long ways out from the planet. From the sensor signal, they had pinged the planet and the inner system pretty hard while they waited for their drives to recharge.

Javier didn't know the exact model of ship coming, but

that was a commercial scanner pulse, and not anything military. Nor a Particularly good one, either.

He assumed a dead-average everything for the freighter, and then down-graded that assumption by ten percent, them being smugglers. Only the military ever had enough money to keep everything tuned, unless you could bribe techs at bases with fresh fruit cobbler, like Javier always had.

Back when *Mielikki* had a full botany station growing things year round.

Back before Sokolov had turned him into a slave.

Even *Janissary* was just a fancy title for what he did.

Javier flipped a coin in his head, then went ahead and brought the ship back to full readiness with a triple bell.

Sykora was already watching him like a hawk, but she nodded, then took the time to fold up her knitting carefully, instead of stuffing it randomly into the bag so she could get to one of her pistols quickly.

The woman was a violent psychopath, but she was a professional about it.

Sokolov emerged from his office about the same moment the passive scanners picked up a new signal and beeped intermittently until Javier silenced the alarm.

"What do we have?" the captain asked as he took his grand chair.

Other crew filed in at the same time. Warfare might be imminent. Or plunder.

"Commercial freighter," Javier replied, reading the signals the intruder was happily emitting. "I'm guessing a Kallasky Engineering Mark IV *Windwagon*, when she originally rolled off the factory floor."

"And Creator only knows what she looks like now," Zakhar said.

If there was a more customizable light freighter hull in the galaxy, Javier hadn't met it. Kallasky had made this model to be turned into almost anything a new owner desired. And do so cheaply, with whole modules that could be plucked out like seeds and interchanged from a standard parts catalog.

"She should have been in for a major engine tune at least six months ago," Javier said, studying the readouts.

For a supposed pirate/smuggler, the vessel was a wealth of signals intelligence. Most of it was garbage, but the sheer volume said something.

Mostly that they weren't trying to hide.

Which really did not leave Javier with a good feeling.

From the looks of the people around him, they agreed.

"What do we have?" Zakhar asked.

"She's above us now," Javier said. "Her last jump was conservative, and she's moving down to insert into an equatorial orbit, but doing it slowly."

"Any sign of a second vessel?" Zakhar inquired.

"None," Javier replied. "You're sure these people are supposed to be smugglers?"

"That was the task we were assigned," Zakhar said.

Javier nodded, but mostly as a placeholder.

Assigned.

He already knew that while Zakhar Sokolov owned the pocket warship, the man also belonged to what the more lurid news organizations liked to call *Pirate Clans*. If you had the money, the connections, and the need, you could hire *Storm Gauntlet* to do things, usually with plausible deniability.

One of these days, Javier decided, he might need to know a great deal more about how that whole underworld thing worked.

Rather than ask another stupid question, Javier routed one of his screens over to Sokolov's station. He watched the captain look down and study it intently for almost a minute.

Zakhar finally looked up with a very sour taste in the set of his mouth.

"The name *Calypso* mean anything to you?" Javier asked in an innocent voice.

He watched Zakhar look the name of the vessel up in the encyclopedia.

"Greek myth?" the captain asked.

"That's the origin," Javier agreed. "It's also a fairly common name for ships engaged in scientific research. Aquatic, predating starflight. Transponder identifies the ship as the property of the University of *Uelkal*."

"Considering how much someone paid for us to be here, I can't imagine a screw-up of that magnitude slipping through," Zakhar observed. "So you're probably right and it might be a trap."

Javier nodded grimly.

There were times when he would have settled for being wrong. This was one of them.

Zakhar nodded as well.

"Nav, when they get into their orbit, hide us above them in the gravity well, full stealth," he said. "If they move, notify me. Otherwise, we'll wait to see who shows up to play."

***

THE TEA MUG appeared at his right hand, almost by magic.

Javier refused to look, though; fully aware that the ship was still inhabited by evil pixies, carefully disguised as wardroom stewards.

Green tea from the color. Chewy, from the way it seemed to swirl with its own whirlpool when he finally looked down.

Javier steeled himself.

He took a sip. Perfection, itself.

Javier knew he was doomed.

A day had passed since *Calypso* had made orbit. *Storm Gauntlet* perched above them, like a hawk on a thermal hunting an oblivious pigeon.

The only thing that had broken the monotony was the amount of sensor data he had added, as *Calypso* had spent their whole time pinging the planet loudly with a sensor package almost as good as the pirate had.

The planet was dead as a doorknob. No question about it. But Javier could have done a full survey thesis just from his notes in the last twenty-four hours. It gave him something to do while he waited for that other shoe to drop. Everybody forgot how dull the waiting bits could be, even if you were walking a tightrope over a lava bed.

His board chirped happily. Around him, the skeleton bridge crew woke up from whatever they were doing.

After a moment, the guy watching the gunnery boards nodded at him. He was a tall, gawky kid with dark, brown skin and instincts almost as good as Sykora's. Just the person to babysit the big guns while they waited for something.

"Breakaway confirmed, sir," Thomas Obasanjo said. "*Calypso* has launched a shuttle."

Javier sounded the summons.

Sykora had apparently been in the day office with Sokolov, as she emerged one step behind him and took up her station.

"Good news," Javier smiled his most innocent smile at the giant woman.

"I doubt it," she sneered back at him.

"Oh, no," Javier disagreed with a smile. "They just launched a shuttle that's headed for the surface. You might get to go down and shoot people."

The way her eyes sorta gleamed told Javier all he needed

13

to know about the woman's state of mind. Just as frustrated at the inactivity as he was, but at least she had a hope of being able to do something.

Nobody was going to rescue *The Science Officer*. Not even evil, wardroom pixies.

"I thought you said there was nothing down there, mister," Sokolov prodded.

"There isn't," Javier agreed. "And I've just spent a day reading their scanner logs to prove it."

"How did you read their scanner logs?" another voice intruded as she entered the bridge from another hatch.

Mary-Elizabeth Suzuki. Gunner extraordinaire. Dark hair and dark eyes. Lousy poker player. Pretty good dancer.

"I know what frequency they pulse on," Javier replied as he watched her walk. She was tall and skinny and a joy to watch move, or hold dancing. "That same signal comes back and we can capture it. I know enough major surface features now that everyone on both crews could have something officially named after them."

"Irrelevant." The captain did his Captain-thing. He speared Javier with an inquisitive eye. "Why?"

"How the hell should I know?" Javier asked. "You're the experts at being pirates. Maybe he has to go bury treasure? You know, *X marks the spot*?"

"Very funny," Sokolov replied.

The captain turned to Sykora, still all spit and polish formalness.

"Djamila," he commanded. "Organize a ground team. We'll pounce on the ship, and Del can insert you on top of them before they can hide or destroy anything."

She got that look in her eyes. Javier knew he was doomed.

"Don't forget your toothbrush, Mister Science Officer," she crooned at him. "You'll be joining us."

Javier already knew that. But he'd also take more than just a toothbrush on this trip.

This might be the day when he finally got to kill that woman.

PART THREE

In his sixty-five years in this galaxy, Delridge Smith had seen and done pretty much everything, he figured. Hell, in most places, the statute of limitations had even expired, but he'd never gotten around to comparing stupid feats with Aritza. Let that poor kid think he was a debaucherous pig. Del still made Javier look like a Nature Scout by comparison, if you went back far enough.

He ran a hand through the gray stubble on his head and then the neat, trimmed, white beard he had affected.

These days, all Del wanted to do was fly. Sokolov had offered him the ultimate gig: piloting a pirate assault shuttle. And letting him decorate it himself. All the adventure and craziness, with far less risk of someone over there being good enough to take him down on anything except luck.

'Cause when your luck was up, that was that.

Everyone else today was wearing gray and green splotch patterns as he looked out from the bridge hatch, down onto the shuttle's transport bay. Good to blend in, down on the surface.

Del's entire wardrobe consisted of baggy gray pants with

pockets on the thighs, and a rainbow of fourteen different bright, floral-print shirts of an ancient style still called *Hawaiian.*

Del watched the science officer organize himself while Sykora and her pathfinders packed guns and backpacks.

Javier had brought the larger of his two drones on this drop.

The armed one.

To an abandoned planet.

Considering how many guns Djamila had, just on her person alone, to say nothing of the rest of her team, Javier didn't need any guns.

Need.

From the look on Aritza's face when he thought nobody was looking, it wasn't an accidental choice.

"Djamila," Del said, getting her attention quietly, even across the noise of people humping bags up the landing ramp of his assault shuttle. "Since this is an unknown situation, I'd feel more comfortable if you were manning the turret on the way down."

She fixed him with a look that just spelled out how little the woman understood poker.

"Del," she replied, almost exasperated. "There's nothing going to jump us. Even Aritza cops to that one."

"Humor an old man" Del implored her politely.

The girl and the science officer, put together, had only a few more years in this sky as Del did himself. And he'd seen a great deal more stupidity and combat than probably most of the crew.

Ah, the adventures of youth. But, any crash you can walk away from, regardless of which mountain you slammed it into first.

Del pulled out his clipboard and started the fourth page

of his pre-flight checklist as Sykora gave a machine gun of orders to her people.

Even Aritza looked curiously in his direction.

Del just smiled serenely. Three more pages to go.

Task complete and landing bay finally settled, Del joined Djamila on the shuttle flight deck and brought the beast to full power.

Delridge Smith only had a few superstitions at this point. The assault shuttle had no name.

None.

Nothing he had flown in the last twenty-five years had gotten a name. All his previous fighters and shuttles, the ones with names, had ended up dead in pieces somewhere. Better to not tempt the Fates on this one. They had apparently appreciated his effort.

And he liked his flight deck decorated like a Merankorr brothel, all pink and frilly, with faux fur and glitter paint on the walls. It went with his loud shirts and the Caribbean music he played, all steel drums and wood pipes.

That comforted him when he was doing crazy things.

Del settled into the flight chair and locked everything in place, both hands on multi-function controls that let him do everything without moving more than ten centimeters.

It was a really excellently designed ship. And tough enough for anything he had tried to put it through. At least so far.

"What are you up do, Del?" Sykora asked over the private comm channel as she brought the turret live and cycled it through its paces.

"You two are fire and oil," Del replied. "I would prefer not making someone clean blood off of my transport deck. You will never get the smell out. Trust me, I've tried."

Give her credit. The dragoon didn't play stupid. They had been comrades for several years now.

"It won't be today, Del," she replied.

"Probably," he agreed. "But I don't ever see you two making peace."

"Why should we?" she snarled at him.

Del knew he was pushing. Only the captain really had an inside gig to talk turkey with the woman, but Del could play the part of the grumpy, old man at least well enough to make her listen.

"Things would be a lot less tense for the rest of us if we weren't worried about becoming collateral damage in your little feud," he replied. "I realize that you two have never noticed that in your blind ambition."

Silence. Hopefully introspection, and not her throwing the headset across the open space as a prelude to stomping up from the gun deck and punching him.

She might do that.

Just in case, Del brought all the power live and stood the little shuttle up on its toes. With any luck, Djamila would stay strapped in until she calmed down.

"Bridge, this is the shuttle," he said into the comm. "Ready whenever you are."

"Roger that, Del," Zakhar replied. "Stand by."

Del watched the feed from the mothership.

Storm Gauntlet was a heavily modified Strike Corvette, an escort upgraded as a squadron leader once upon a time, and then retired out of *Concord* fleet service a generation ago when all the aftermath stopped aftermathing. When old warships like this and old warriors like Del got put on the shore for good.

She was more than enough to handle a single light freighter sitting below her in the gravity well, looking the wrong direction. Just in case, though, Del knew the captain would power everything up and race down at her, waiting for a good, solid firing solution from the Ion Pulsar to completely disable the wee beastie of a vessel, so the big, bad pirates could dock with her and hold her in orbit.

Nothing worse in the world than watching your prize fall out of the sky as all the crew bails out in lifepods and everything you hoped to steal burns up. Nothing more embarrassing, either.

Nothing went wrong today, either.

Hawks on pigeons.

On his primary screen, Del watched *Storm Gauntlet*'s B-Turret, the one with the double ion cannon, light that poor freighter up with fairy fire, a reverse St. Elmo's Fire bringing ruin instead of divine protection from the storm.

"Shuttle, you are clear for launch," Sokolov's voice came over the com. "Good hunting."

Del acknowledged then maneuvered the beast through the shield lock and into open space like a salmon climbing for spawning season.

One quick look at his boards showed nothing in space above him, and only one interesting spot on the entire, damned planet, roughly forty degrees south latitude on the leeward side of a big continent.

The spot where *Calypso*'s shuttle had gone to ground.

Del pushed the nose of the vessel over and jammed the throttle open. Assault shuttles were designed to go hot through an atmosphere.

Let's get you before you get away, and see what secrets you have to hide.

PART FOUR

Javier had felt the shuttle powering up, back up on the ship, and deliberately pulled every one of his straps extra tight. Del Smith probably thought the look in his eyes was reassuring.

Javier knew better.

The atmosphere had parted like the Red Sea, under protest, wailing like a hungry *ban sidhe* on a dusty, August night as Del took her in hot and crazy.

Not a surprise. Del was already crazy.

On the feed from the flight deck, the marble turned into a map, and then a skyscraper's window. Perched on the edge of a cold promontory overlooking a vast, icy valley.

From this approach, Javier could see the big, flat ledge, about halfway up one of the mountains that made up the basin. And the cave that appeared to open up behind it.

There was a small cargo shuttle nose-out and butt-in on that ledge, but no movement Javier could see.

And considering how sneaky the Assault Shuttle was swooping, those folks might not know there was anything wrong down there, other than sudden silence from orbit as *Calypso* went dark.

"Landing party, this is your captain speaking," Del's bored voice emerged from the speakers. "Please stow your gear and place your tray tables in the upright and locked position. Our target appears to be cold, and we will be on the ground in ninety seconds."

Javier settled for popping his knuckles and beeping Suvi to make sure she wasn't locked into one of her video games, ignoring the outside world.

"Are we there yet?" scrolled across his board on the little remote's controller with a sad face.

Javier's cover story, of upgrading and automating his pair of survey drones to make them more autonomous, worked to let her have to spend less time pretending to be listening to him, and more time flying. At the same time, they still had to make sure nobody realized she was in there.

If Sokolov found out, Javier was most likely a dead man and she would be a slave.

"Almost," Javier typed back. "Prepare for high winds and precipitation."

"You stay warm," she sent.

Trust his AI sidekick to go all motherly on him when they set down on a new planet.

But Javier checked anyway. A mask with supplemental oxygen hung around his neck, just in case. The warm suit under his pants and jacket was currently dialed up halfway, since Del had kept the landing bay chilly.

Javier went ahead and dialed the suit up to compensate for zero degrees Centigrade outside. The change wouldn't be instant. However, it would be enough to keep him warm when they got on the ground.

Everything else was in his backpack for now, except the "flight controller" for the drone hanging on his belt.

Adding a "voice controller" function just meant he could talk out loud, not that Suvi would answer with people around.

A good-enough halfway measure today.

Impact.

Del must be feeling his oats today.

Usually, Del's landings were feather soft. This was one hard, and the bay door was already halfway down.

At least the dragoon hadn't felt the need to light the shuttle up with her cannon as she got close.

Javier would have lost that bet.

Sykora came pounding down the steps from the flight deck at a fast jog, pausing just long enough to count noses before she went down the ramp into the bitter cold at a dead run, battle rifle out. Both pathfinders ran behind her: Sascha with the nice hips and Hajna with the long legs. Half-a-dozen male gun-bunnies followed, apparently intent on invading Guatemala.

"Probe. Access Command Mode," Javier said aloud, just in case anybody was listening besides him. Del was the only person still on the ship. "Exit shuttle and begin scanning. Defensive perimeter, please."

Translation: Make sure nobody is sneaking up on us. Shoot them if they do.

Javier unbuckled and stood slowly, stretching everything as Del appeared.

"Not in a rush?" the ancient pilot drawled.

"Let her absorb any incoming fire," Javier replied, slinging his pack. "They aren't going anywhere. I'm just here for buried treasure."

"Come again?" Del asked.

"Long story," Javier cast over his shoulder as he shouldered the backpack and tromped down the ramp, happily last.

Suvi hovered overhead in her dangerous little globe, like the eye of doom.

Calypso's shuttle wasn't smoking, so they had apparently opened the door at the top of the ramp, instead of blowing it apart with explosives.

You never knew with these yahoos.

One man guarded Del's hatch. Another protected *Calypso*'s shuttle. Javier assumed the rest were aboard the other ship, scaring people.

They were good at that.

Something caused him to look to his left as he emerged. Buried treasure, maybe.

Pirates always needed a secret place to hide things.

X marks the spot.

The cave was only about forty meters deep. There was a bank vault door back there, fit for *Jotunheim*.

Seriously, seventeen, maybe twenty meters high. Ten wide. Turning on Javier-sized hinge pins.

And completely invisible to all the scans he had done or intercepted from orbit.

Groovy.

Javier ignored everyone else and wandered that direction. The dragoon and her mob could catch up. Plus, Suvi was faster and more dangerous than Djamila Sykora, on any day.

Not much snow in the cave, for all the slushy ugliness out on the ledge. Mostly what swirling winds might deposit if left to their own devices, like a bored eight-year-old.

However, any snow that remained had been scraped off to one side when that giant door had swung open recently. Like, say, in the last hour, probably about the time that the assault shuttle had slowed down to sub-sonic speeds as it got close.

Javier wandered close. Ambled, more or less.

He wasn't willing to admit that the door impressed

him. Not after trying to figure out how to steal the *Land Leviathan*, but his subconscious mind kept wanting to show him the evil giants lurking on the other side of that huge door, just waiting for a little mouse named Javier to knock.

Not a single beanstalk in sight.

At least the door controls were at a human scale, off on the right side. Simple little ten-key keypad, with individual buttons the size of his palm. Javier assumed they were meant to be pushed by hands in mitts, or handy elbows.

And someone had etched the control sequence into the metal panel just above the numbers. Obviously, it was meant to be opened by strangers who were intelligent, while keeping wildlife outside.

Briefly, he wondered why nobody had put a *Sentience* in the system, but then he remembered where he was.

Even the most carefully programmed AI would go utterly nuts from boredom given enough time alone.

Nope. Better to have a stupid system here, and rely on humans.

Was it well-enough engineered that some future star-faring species might come along and open the thing? Humanity hadn't found anything more sophisticated than lichens and simple plant life, anywhere, but that didn't mean nobody else was coming along.

Fermi might have been wrong today, but the galaxy was a big place and forever was a long time.

The flight controls on his hip chirped.

"Should we wait for the dragon lady? It might be dangerous, or something," Suvi typed with all the sarcastic insolence he had programmed into her.

Javier grinned and typed.

"Buried treasure, young lady," he typed back. "What if I don't want to share with the other pirates?"

His reward was a blinking smiley face, flickering quickly and randomly around the spectrum.

Truly, Suvi could be a goof.

Javier keyed the four digit sequence and listened as heavy bolts slowly retracted into the mountainside. The door began to move slowly outward beside him.

What was the worst that could happen?

PART FIVE

ZAKHAR HAD BEEN way more adventurous in his youth.

Time was, he would have been happy to swap Javier places and go romp around on a strange planet looking for treasure and having adventures.

Becoming a starship captain, and then an entrepreneur, had cured him of some of his crazier ideas.

Okay, maybe tempered them enough so that he could live vicariously through the stories of other people getting shot at and nearly falling off cliffs.

Dry socks and fresh coffee was a happy trade-off.

It had been two hours since they had captured the freighter. One hour since Del and Djamila had landed and secured the shuttle. *Storm Gauntlet* had undocked from *Calypso*, but left a skeleton crew aboard, having found only three people over there to capture.

Zakhar hadn't let the bridge crew relax from Javier's ideas of paranoid sneakiness, though.

An *Osiris*-class Strike Corvette like *Storm Gauntlet* was only a little warship, as military vessels went. Pulse Cannons in Turret A fore, and Turret X aft for balance. Turret B had been refitted with an Ion Pulsar to capture ships instead of destroying them. Four smaller batteries with twin pulsars as defensive weapons on the front and rear flanks. She was mostly an escort that had been upgraded in service as a squadron leader, but nothing dangerous to big warships.

Hell on wheels against the average freighter, though.

Calypso had been stunned unconscious at the first shot from the Ion Pulsar. Mary-Elizabeth was an expert at that sort of thing. A couple of follow-up shots had just been gilding the lily, but there were no penalties for overkill in this business.

All a victim had to do was randomly trigger their jump drives to escape, even from this deep in a gravity well. It usually got you away, and if you stayed quiet, you probably could buy enough time to repair the drive matrix configurations to escape clean if your engineers were any good.

Smart crews would program an emergency jump for that exact purpose.

Hell, he'd only caught Javier Aritza in the first place because the man had dropped out of a jump almost on top of *Storm Gauntlet* and was stuck in the middle of recharging.

Bad luck for Javier. Maybe good luck for Zakhar.

His crew had been almost as broken down as their ship when the science officer first came aboard. Zakhar looked out over his bridge and considered what life might be like as a retired, former pirate.

Javier fixing the life support system had injected a spark into the crew that had been missing. Since then, he had become an officer that the crew would follow.

Now, if I can only figure out how to get him to stay after he has paid off his debt, which is coming up all too soon. Maybe I'll charge him extra to buy back his chickens and arboretum. Something.

Zakhar day-dreamed about taking a desk job somewhere.

Anywhere.

Someplace where he wasn't a pirate warlord, a slaver, and a wanted criminal. Maybe take Djamila with him and sell the ship to Javier, so those two could finally be separated and not have to kill each other.

A person could dream, right?

"Sir," a voice intruded on Zakhar's happy little fantasy.

Tobias Gibney. Gunner's Mate. Also, pretty damned good with the sensors when Javier wasn't around. He was short, skinny, and pale. And so quiet about his past that nobody knew anything about the man, except which planets he adamantly refused to ever take leave on.

Zakhar looked over.

Gibney had an angry look on his face, but it seemed to be pointed inward. It usually was.

"Go," Zakhar prompted.

"I've got a weird signal return," Gibney finally said. "I'd say a sensor ghost, but I know how good our scanners are. Science Officer would have spotted something going that far off beam a while ago and fixed it."

Yeah, Javier would have.

Not much brought out the nerdy professionalism in that man. Having better eyes and ears than any warship in service was high on that list, though.

Zakhar checked his boards. Everything was still in stealth mode, passive sensors only, but drinking in as much data as they could and filtering it according to the paranoid tendencies of one Mister Javier Aritza.

The chances of a false positive were technically above zero, but not by enough to actually count in anything but horseshoes and hand grenades.

"Where?" Zakhar asked in a tight voice.

Once upon a time, he had been a captain in the *Concord* Fleet. Warrior. Commander.

Right sneaky bastard.

Being a pirate hadn't taken any of that away from him.

Calypso was orbiting in front of them as they went, a little below and off the port bow. A silvery object close enough to be a very detailed model on a twenty-zoom telescope, but not so close as to present a maneuvering risk.

Good ship handling was still one of Sokolov's hallmarks.

"Higher plane. Sixteenth of an orbit ahead," Gibney chopped off his syllables like slicing carrots.

A-yup. Right where I'd want to be to start an attack pass. If I was running silent and trying to get close enough to ambush someone. Come to a dead stop relative to everything and let them come up under me before I uncloaked.

A genius admiral had once said that the difference between a good commander and a great one was fifteen seconds.

Which meant reacting immediately instead of dithering.

"Comm," Zakhar snapped his command voice across the entire bridge. "Break radio silence and order *Calypso* to emergency jump and then go silent. Bring all shields to maximum settings now."

"That will void our cloak, sir," the comm yeoman stated.

"Acknowledged," Zakhar said. "Tell Del to go silent as well. Nav, as soon as *Calypso* confirms, trigger our jump. Up and out. Get me clear so Engineering can start putting us back together. Drop us back to full cloak and total silence as soon as we come out of jump."

Things started happening immediately, at least here.

Calypso blinked out of existence. The ship was in good-enough shape, and the crew over there capable. They could get it all to rights in a couple of hours. Three or four light-hours of empty space took a long time to quarter, if you were looking for a silent needle in an empty haystack.

Storm Gauntlet surged with power as every generator was suddenly dropped into line and paralleled.

Above and ahead, *something* appeared. The mystery bird got off one salvo that hit home on the shields with a mighty sledgehammer, but not a second one. Not the dangerous one.

And then *Storm Gauntlet* jumped.

Darkness.

Emptiness.

Otherspace.

Back.

Everything went back to dimness as *Storm Gauntlet*'s crew hid, silent mice in the cupboard. Down below, Engineering would be a kicked-over ant's nest of activity as the jump matrix went sideways from too much gravity, too close. An average crew could fix it in six hours. On an average day his Chief Engineer, Andreea Dalca could probably do it in three.

Hopefully, this was a better-than-average day for her.

The captain over there had been good. But he had made a mistake.

I would have fired everything from under the cloak and let it collapse, rather than trying to bring it down cleanly. It would regenerate just as well as the jump matrix.

The difference had been not getting a second, full broadside from a battle frigate-sized Raider. One hit had gotten home hard. The second would have done damage, had Zakhar still been there.

Zakhar checked the readout. He even knew the vessel that had tried to kill them.

Ajax.

One of the enforcers for Walvisbaai Industrial.

Officially, the competition.

If the many pirate clans could be arrayed on a spectrum from good to evil, Zakhar would put his bosses, the Jarre Foundation, somewhere closer to the nice end.

Walvisbaai was about as bad as it got.

There was no chance in hell that they just happened to be out here in the middle of nowhere, all stealthed up and ready to attack.

Piet glanced over from his pilot's seat, but remained silent. The smile in the man's eyes was enough. He didn't have to actually say it out loud.

Javier had been right.

It was a trap.

BOOK FOURTEEN: SVALBARD

PART ONE

As the humongous door waddled open and lights on a single overhead track came on, Suvi sent a soft ping on a weird, ultrasonic frequency down the big atrium. Just the sort of thing for annoying the hell out of bats.

She didn't figure there were any on this planet, anyway. And if there were, better to find out what sort of mean bastards might have colonized an iceball in the middle of nowhere, early, right?

Tunnel. Straight for a bit, back into the soul of the mountain. Inclined at exactly seven degrees for the four hundred meters she could scan. Either the tunnel hairpinned at that point, or there was another door blocking things.

Because the outside air was just at freezing, she had transformed her regular black, skin-tight, leather flying-suit gear into fur-lined pants, snow goggles, and a parka made from a hideously-pink polar bear.

You could do anything when you were an AI. You just had to dream silly enough.

Suvi maneuvered her armed gunship through the door and looked around. Javier was following her lead, and the corridor was empty, but it was still twenty-seven meters tall, perfectly round if you had cut off the bottom third. Probably bored that way, and then all the pipes and wiring put in underneath before they built a new floor.

Weird, but humans did things that made no sense, even to themselves.

Because she could, Suvi decided to fly this mission on the ceiling. She left fourteen centimeters of clearance above her, tilted her nose down and imitated one of those flying cops tracking speeders with a radar gun as she moved at Javier's relaxed pace.

And because there might be carnivorous bats around, she unlocked the pop-up pulse pistol turret the bigger drone had on the bottom ring. Probably heavy enough to knock a moose on his ass.

Girl needed to be prepared.

The big cathedral door began to close behind them with a hooting sound, probably designed to remind stupid humans to move out of the way. She had to dial down her audio sensors a little, and throw in a filter, or it would have been extra annoying. Kinda the reverse of what she had just done to the bats.

Javier was mostly watching her feed as she let every scanner and probe she had make as much noise as it wanted. She hadn't found anyone, so if they were here, they were really good at hiding.

Or they were ghosts.

She was pretty sure none of Javier's wardroom pixies had followed him here.

Not yet, anyway.

"Anything?" Javier asked.

"Moles don't tunnel straight," she typed back. "Space dragons?"

That got a laugh out of him, which was good. Javier had

been too tense lately. Probably needed to get laid more. You never knew with organics, but that seemed to be his go-to remedy, since he didn't drink with nearly the audacity of some of his old stories.

Thirty seconds after the outer door closed, the light flickered out, but Javier had apparently been expecting it. He had a flashlight out and on. Good enough for him to see, and she didn't need to add anything.

The inner door, when they got there, was just as grandiose as the outer one. In better shape, since it didn't have the added exposure, but cut to exactly the same dimensions. Someone had forged both simultaneously and put them here.

What the hell did you hide on a dying planet in the middle of nowhere? And why would it need to be this big?

Suvi took a quick spin through the encyclopedia she had finally convinced Javier to upload, but nothing jumped out with an answer.

Javier approached the inner door and took off his gloves as she watched. He stashed the flight controller in his backpack and studied the big door.

Hmm. Temperature was warmer here. Already three degrees ambient, and the door itself was nine degrees. Was there a volcano on the other side of that wall, or something?

Javier stepped to the side and entered a different four-digit sequence to open this portal.

Interesting that they didn't use the same one as the outer.

No, strike that. Absolutely illogical. And thus, human.

The door beeped once and started to open.

The hallway lights came on again.

Because she was above it, Suvi had a great view of the interior, while still being kinda invisible up here.

And that was good, since there were a dozen guys on the inside, armed to the teeth.

Javier had no chance to move before he was suddenly at the wrong end of the problem, but at least he never looked up at her. And the visible guns were all stun models, as near as she could tell.

"Don't move," one of the closest guys said.

"Yeah, I kinda figured that," he replied.

"Who are you?" the stranger asked.

"Just a guy," Javier said.

And then they shot him.

PART TWO

THE JUMP HADN'T BEEN as far as Zakhar had hoped.

Hopefully, it was still far enough.

That was the problem with triggering an emergency jump. By its very nature, it would be a random distance, in a random direction, since the drives were not capable of factoring the extreme curvature of space-time once you got too close to a planet.

Still, it had worked.

Storm Gauntlet had gotten clear before *Ajax* was able to lock on and hit hard enough to get through the shields.

However, now was when things got dangerous.

Calypso would be staying as dark as a hole in space, waiting either for orders, or to make their escape if *Ajax* took out *Storm Gauntlet*. Either way, he didn't have to worry about them. An unarmed freighter had no business being around here, so they would be moving away as quietly as they could. He'd already set up a rendezvous with the prize crew, for exactly this sort of surprise.

At the same time, the ground team was trapped on a very hostile planet. With an enemy overhead.

Zakhar wasn't sure if their best outcome would be to be abandoned here forever, or to be captured by a bunch of goons from Walvisbaai. Certain death versus the possibility of something worse.

The control boards, at least, were promising.

Engineering was on the ball. Drive tuning would be accurate within an acceptable limit in under an hour. Piet was flying. Mary-Elizabeth had the guns. Even Gibney was doing nearly as good a job as Javier at the science officer station.

And now, to sail into harm's way, against an invisible opponent.

"Ahead one quarter," Zakhar ordered. Just enough to get them in the right direction, having already killed their inertia.

Time to get sneaky.

Zakhar studied the various readouts at his fingertips.

Ajax had been a purpose-built pirate ship, rather than a retired and refurbished old warboat like *Storm Gauntlet*. She was bigger and meaner, but most assuredly not built to the same standards for durability. That was expensive to engineer and fabricate, and like most pirate ships, *Ajax* would be relying on an overabundance of firepower for such a small hull.

Hell, at the end of the day, *Ajax* could probably go toe-to-toe with a destroyer for a little bit, before the bigger ship's mass began to tell. But that wouldn't do Zakhar any good today. These two vessels were capable of pounding each other into scrap at a fairly even pace. Sykora and Aritza were still trapped on the planet below.

The edge he had was in his sensors. Already, Gibney had managed to spot the other vessel once. After all, the cloak function wasn't perfect, nor invulnerable. Just an energy shield that masked nearly all emissions behind a blanket of randomness.

Nearly being the operative phrase here.

Could they do it again?

Zakhar's ability to rescue Djamila, from this trap he had stepped into, hinged on it.

What was the best way to out-think the other guy?

Zakhar glanced over at Gibney, face down and studying everything intently, as if Javier was leaning over his shoulder offering suggestions.

Yeah, there was an inspiration.

When in doubt, do something crazy.

"Piet," Zakhar continued, as if not a moment had passed. "Plot an insertion orbit that runs on an oblong angle."

"How oblong?" the pilot actually looked over his shoulder with a concerned face.

"Del landed forty degrees south?" Zakhar asked.

Piet nodded carefully.

"So forty-five south, fifty-five north," Zakhar concluded. "And keep it extremely high."

Just the unconscious recoil that shook Piet's whole body told Zakhar just how offended a well-trained pilot would be with such a course. Which was the whole point. He would never think of something like this on his own, so he wouldn't be expecting it.

Out-think the other guy.

Everyone else plotted orbits that ran parallel with the equatorial plane, usually at some latitude that put you directly overhead of some important terrestrial target below you. That or an orbital insertion that let you cover the whole planet as you went pole-to-pole with it turning beneath you.

This was the sort of thing Javier would have thought up.

"Why this orbit, sir?" Gibney asked, trying to wrap his

head around the kind of craziness that usually emanated from the science corner of the bridge.

Probably afraid it was contagious.

"I want him to fly below us at some point, Tobias," Zakhar replied. "Our sensors are better than his, so if we can get him to shadow part of the planet, we'll see him."

"Then what?" Mary-Elizabeth chimed in from the gunner station.

"Still working on that part," Zakhar said. "Feel free to offer ideas."

"Roger that," she replied.

Zakhar opened an internal comm channel.

"Wardroom," he said quietly. "Prepare to feed the bridge crew lunch and dinner in place, please."

He closed the channel and got to thinking.

How do you beat a bigger enemy, when all he has to do is just stop you from saving your people?

PART THREE

UNLIKE DEL'S ASSAULT SHUTTLE, the pilot from *Calypso*'s shuttle hadn't stayed aboard after the other group had landed.

Or if he had, he had found a really good place to hide. One even Djamila couldn't find.

She finally considered it good enough, for now.

Her team had cleared the vessel about as quickly as anyone could have managed. Certainly, they would have been on the podium, if this had been a competitive event. The after-action report wouldn't have many deductions.

She left Sascha and Hajna aboard the vessel as a precaution and went outside to gather up the strike team. The two girls were good scouts and pathfinders, but the six boys were more linear.

The men were for the times when charging a machine gun nest really was the best solution.

Del was standing in the hatchway as she emerged back into the brisk air.

"Where's Aritza?" she called, looking around.

He smiled at her, and pointed back to the tunnel.

Damn it. Was that man incapable of ever acting like an

adult?

"Lock everything up, Del," she ordered, signaling her men to join her, battle rifle held casually pointed downrange.

The first door was better suited to be a flight hangar, even if it was built like a bank vault, except that it was just too narrow for anything big enough to be dangerous. Still, someone was obviously intent on hiding something down here, or it would have shown up on scanners.

Aritza wouldn't have been capable of keeping out if he saw something like this. Just like he wasn't capable of not walking right into what was obviously a trap, instead of waiting for backup.

Hopefully, he had finally met with that tragic accident she had always been meaning to arrange, whatever Del thought to the contrary.

Six men, and her. Good enough.

Everyone was prepared. Del had already started withdrawing the landing ramp upwards. Aritza's sensor drone would be nice about now, but had obviously gone inside the deathtrap with him.

Hopefully, it had survived enough that she could make use of it in the future. After he was dead.

The panel was obvious. Human designed. Set into a stone façade. Door opening outward from a plug frame, where outside overpressure would just drive it deeper into a narrowing face and let it survive much greater pressures than just resting in place would allow.

Good architecture for defense.

She checked the keypad and noted that someone had permanently carved a four-digit numeric sequence above it.

Her men had squatted into a defensive formation. Well spread-out against grenades. Covering front, sides, and rear. Every weapon was hot, judging from the fingers carefully not touching triggers.

She moved to one side and pressed her bottom flat against the cold wall. Given the confines, Djamila slung her rifle and drew the pistol on her hip. She transferred it to her left hand, multi-dimensional ambidexterity having always been one of her greatest assets, and keyed the button sequence with her right.

The behemoth beeped and began to open.

Inside, Djamila found a vast cathedral empty. Her men were strung out behind her as they moved, carefully covering everything.

The overhead light falling dark was a surprise, but only for a moment. Lights on barrel rails came on, as well as the one on Djamila's pistol. It made everyone a target, but there wasn't much they could do, unless they wanted to abandon the science officer, or go back for night gear.

Leaving that punk would have been a happy solution, but she still had to find the crew that had come down with the shuttle in the first place. Knowing Aritza, he had already found them and was drinking and having a wild, uproarious time.

Fortunately, the corridor had smooth walls, so nothing was in a position to ambush them, unless they came from a hidden door. And her men were just waiting for that.

It didn't feel like a home, the kind with comfortable side corridors. More like a doomsday vault, where *Neu Berne* High Command had once burrowed into a mountain to hide from orbital strikes that had never come.

Almost half a kilometer in, Djamila found a second vault door, an identical copy of the first, athwart her path in the darkness.

A woman's voice came out of the dark sky.

"Dragoon Sykora," Djamila heard a modulated voice that almost sounded like an angel. "You are in extreme danger."

PART FOUR

JAVIER ALWAYS FOUND it hard to distinguish between a good, morning-after hangover, and getting blasted unconscious with a commercial stun rifle. Strange ceilings, weird smells, and total strangers around him didn't help sort anything out.

"Where am I?" he groaned.

Maybe groaned.

It might have come out as a general blur of syllables. That was a common side effect of both kinds of mornings.

"Ah, you are awake," a man's cheery voice cut through the gunk coating Javier's mind.

Javier opened his eyes anyway.

A fat, cheery elf with a white beard hovered in the air above him.

No, leaned over.

I'm flat on my back on the floor.

The pain was fading, so Javier leaned towards the stunner theory. A hangover that good usually lasted a day or so.

"Who are you?" Javier strung syllables together as he sat up, pulled more or less into a sitting position by the elf.

"Dr. Alex Mornan," the annoyingly-joyful elf replied as he turned into a middle-aged, pudgy, pale-skinned Anglo. "Chief Scientist aboard the Star Yacht *Calypso*. And you might be?"

Calypso?

They were in a small room with a dozen other folks, a big conference table, gray stone walls, and what looked like a locked door.

Oh. Crap. Quadruple cross, at least.

"Navarre," Javier lied.

He needed to have a life after piracy. The fewer people that could connect one Javier Aritza with acts worthy of execution by *Concord* authorities, the better.

"Have you any idea what might be the affair with our erstwhile captors?" Mornan asked.

It took Javier's semi-scrambled brains a second to parse all that back into something comprehensible. It didn't make any sense a second time, either, but he remembered the hard look in the eyes of man who had been hiding inside the vault, just before that jackass pulled the trigger.

"It's a trap," Javier said finally. "We were lured here under false pretenses. What are you doing here?"

False enough pretenses. Ambush a freighter. Hijack the cargo. Get paid.

Obviously, someone had other plans.

"I see," the elf said dubiously. "We were making our annual delivery to the vault, and were greatly surprised to find armed men waiting for us. We've been locked in this compartment for over an hour now. Were you with them?"

"Vault?" Javier asked innocently. "My brain is still scrambled. What's in the vault?"

"Seeds, my good man," Mornan replied. "The future of galactic ecology. This is *Svalbard*. We're standing in the Doomsday Vault."

Seriously? That *wasn't* an old wives tale?

Javier had heard rumors of such a thing. Empty, habitable world. Mountain hollowed out and filled with every kind of plant seed known to humans, regularly updated so that no earth-derived species ever went extinct.

He had joked about raiding the place, back when he was flying survey jobs for the *Concord Fleet*, just to expand his arboretum.

Apparently, it really existed.

Who knew?

"*Svalbard*?" Javier faked. "Of course. My pardon for the holes those pirates seemed to have left in my memory."

"Smashing, my dear chap," Mornan beamed. "What brought you here?"

Javier let the older man pull him the rest of the way to his feet as he thought furiously. The others watched, but stepped back, like he was in the ring with the smaller man.

Not a happy vision, but not much he could do about it.

"There were rumors…" Javier let his voice trail off. "I have been working on a variant of a Terran gooseberry that fixes a variety of useful trace vitamins and minerals with just enough of a secondary euphoric that eating a handful guarantees the average human blissful sleep without narcotic side effects or withdrawal. It dries with seventy percent potency, as well as surviving fermentation that yields a low alcohol wine perfect for long-term shipping."

Javier was able to identify the five professional botanists in the group by the rapt attention they paid, while the others seemed to glaze over at his words.

Always know your audience.

"Go on," Mornan had lost his reserve and leaned forward breathlessly.

"I've bred the root stock too narrowly," Javier admitted with a flash of guilt in his tones. "I was hoping to find something here that was hardy in an 8A climate so that I could cross-pollinate without hybridizing the daughter generations, to stabilize the breed. Then I take it to an agricultural university as a breeding project."

"What are your berries like?" a woman on his left asked sharply.

It suddenly felt like he was defending a thesis. Might be.

"Shockingly pink," Javier grinned at her. "About the size of a good table grape, up to possibly a snooker ball if growth conditions are perfect. Four seeds symmetrically arrayed from the center. Good, juicy flesh. Skin firm enough to handle transport, without being so thick that it turns into a pain to bite through."

"Have you considered…" she started to say, when the door opened.

The man with the hard eyes was standing there. He pointed an angry finger at Javier.

"You," he commanded. "Come with me."

Javier shrugged and turned to the elf.

"Dr. Mornan, it has been a pleasure to meet you," he said. "Pardon me. I'll be back as soon as I can."

The scientist nodded with a sad smile, but kept his silence.

Javier could see the wheels turning in his eyes, though.

Outside, Javier found the rest of the office. Apparently, he had been stashed in the boardroom, because there were a dozen desks around the walls, patiently waiting for people to give them purpose.

And half-a-dozen armed goons.

At least they were professional, with everyone acting sane. Hell, only three of the guys even had guns pointed at him. That had to be a bonus.

It wasn't like he was Sykora, willing and probably capable of taking on all of them at once. And probably winning.

That woman was absolutely a High Priestess of Death, or something.

"Sit," the jackass commanded sharply.

Javier complied. Neither Sykora nor Suvi were here, so these poor bastards were already so badly outnumbered they wouldn't even know it was coming.

"So," Javier even smiled. "You guys are the trap?"

That was apparently the way to back-foot the jackass. His angry scowl turned puzzled. Then cleared up.

"That's right," he agreed. "You're Navarre."

It wasn't a question. Javier didn't figure much of this would be open to debate.

"Correct," he said. "Who hired you folks?"

The jackass's eyes turned to slits. Probably not expecting a formal, polite pirate. Especially not if they had warned him to expect a psychopathic killer like Navarre supposedly was. Probably all set to torture him for information.

"You pissed off a number a folks," Jackass said. "But Slavkov put up the bulk of the funds."

It took Javier a moment to place the name.

Valko Neofit Slavkov. Owner of the *Land Leviathan*, the galaxy's largest rolling resort yacht.

Man, he must be really pissed about being called a moron. And not getting delivered a mass casualty incident when he went to all the effort to hire Navarre in the first place.

Of course, to date, the only people Navarre had killed had been pirates. And they had it coming.

Much like Jackass and his friends here.

"So what's your play?" Javier asked.

Five drachma ante, punk. Jacks or better to open.

"Bounty on your head, alive," Jackass sneered. "Sokolov, either way. Slavkov wants to talk to you, personally."

Good. That gave Javier a whole range of options, if they

wanted to transport him alive somewhere. Assuming they didn't just stun him, drop him into a medically-induced coma, and throw him into a life-support pod for the trip.

Being functionally dead would make escaping a real pain in the ass.

Before Javier could say anything, an alarm began to beep. Javier presumed the inner vault door based the sound.

Jackass looked over his shoulder, cursed under his breath, and turned.

"Stash him," the man commanded as everyone was suddenly armed.

Another of the goons motioned for Javier to stand and pointed him back to where the scientists were currently being held.

Since the alternative was getting stunned and dragged, Javier went willingly.

He wanted to be awake to see what Sykora did to these punks.

PART FIVE

THIS WAS the part that utterly and irrevocably sucked.

Suvi carefully flipped on her running lights and descended from the ceiling, being the target of seven different weapons.

And she couldn't even shoot them all, like she wanted.

Worse, she needed them. Dragon Lady most of all.

And they needed to believe she was an autonomous probe with less brains than a goldfish, or someone might get the bright idea of who was really hiding in here.

"Probe. Access Command Mode," Sykora said, proving that she had been paying attention back on *Shangdu*. "Provide situational map."

Suvi was glad she thought at several thousand times the speed of the average human. And had access to a good encyclopedia. The gap while she figured out what the hell the giant woman was asking was probably long enough for organics to notice.

Stupid, paranoid gun-bunnies.

Still, you didn't make bricks without straw. And even worse pirates than these had the boss captive.

Suvi settled at chest-level on the giant woman and set her running lights in a low-glow pattern. Mostly enough to outline her as a giant, disembodied eyeball.

Maybe she could get Javier to take her trick-or-treating next year?

Suvi used her projector to display a map of the hallway they were in, the door, and as much of the hallway beyond it as she had scanned when the vault was open.

Plus a dozen red X marks for bad men with guns.

She followed that up with a quick video of the ambush, Javier standing still and getting stunned.

"Are there others beyond the door?" Sykora asked.

Suvi caught a twinkle of mischief in the woman's eyes. Javier was right, she really did suck at poker.

Best to modulate the voice.

Suvi found something that sounded like a bad AI special effect from a late-night movie.

"Data insufficient," she replied in the most boring, mechanical voice she could manage.

"Project the image of the shooter again," Sykora commanded.

Hey, how about a little politeness here, lady?

"Please," the Amazon followed up.

Huh. Okay. Old dogs, new tricks. I can play, too.

Suvi put a still scan into three dimensional projection. She could do that with the latest round of updates. It made chess with Javier way more fun.

"Pay attention," Sykora seemed to be talking to her men. "Note that they were all holding stun pistols at the moment of engagement, but every one of them has a lethal weapon either slung across their back, or as a compact carbine. Everyone shift to stun weapons now."

Suvi watched the men rotate through their arsenal wordlessly. Sykora holstered the one on her hip and drew from the shoulder rig.

"Stun grenades?" one of the men asked.

"Sonic only," Sykora replied. "We'll assume that they'll hear the door opening and be prepared for aerosolized gas attack. I would be."

"Roger that."

EVERY SINGLE ONE OF THEM pulled out a grenade from a pouch and held it in their off-hand.

Are you people all that crazy? Who invades an empty planet with that much casual firepower?

"Probe, you are armed, correct?" Sykora asked.

Does the sun rise in the east, lady?

"Affirmative," the machine voice replied monotonously.

"Do you have a stun setting?" Sykora continued.

"Affirmative."

Gods, talk about a boring conversationalist.

"Am I authorized to give you firing instructions?"

Oh, sneaky. And smart enough to assume that Javier might lock someone, ESPECIALLY YOU, out of using the dangerous bits.

"Affirmative."

"Okay," Sykora eyed everyone, including the eye staring back. "They will know the door is opening, and be prepared to ambush us."

Suvi watched the Amazon point to the smallest man present, short for any man when the rest were all well above-average for height and weight.

"You and I will put four grenades through the gap as soon as it opens far enough for a clean entry," Sykora continued. "Everyone else will be flat on the deck and prepared to fire as soon as you have any targets. Stun everything that moves, no questions asked."

Sykora turned and fixed Suvi's chariot with a grim smile.

"Probe. Access Command Mode," Sykora ordered. "From an elevated spot, provide enfilading crossfire on all enemy targets with stun weaponry when the door opens."

"Acknowledged," Suvi said, bored.

If there was a way to make it a fair competition against mere organics, Suvi knew she could run a high score marathon on any flying simulations that included a strafing element, especially the ones with an otherwise-unexplained canyon sequence defended by point turrets. What idiot had thought that one up, anyway?

Open door, standing humans, vertical surprise? Bring it, lady.

Suvi had to give the crazy Dragon Lady credit for pro moves, though. She couldn't remember a single cheesy B-movie she had ever watched where they approached the topic of kicking in a door with anything like what Sykora put together.

Four men, laying or kneeling, pistols covering the opening, while the fifth went clear to the other side and faced rear, in case of a secret door.

Small guy with his butt next to the keypad. Sykora just beyond him. Four grenades in hands.

Sykora looked at everyone individually, including the hammer of the gods overhead.

Suvi flickered her running lights.

"Go," Dragon Lady murmured.

Little Guy keyed the door with his elbow.

Beeps and grinding as the mechanism wound itself up.

Lights came up in the hallway.

Vault door cracked enough to spill light out.

Little Guy leaned in and snapped two grenades through the gap, dropping to one knee and drawing a pistol.

Dragon Lady stepped into a throw and HEAVED her

two grenades like she was gunning the runner down from center field.

Because she could, Suvi tilted her turret down and hovered just above the opening door, painting the room beyond the vault with a scanner pulse hard enough that even humans might feel it.

Anybody wanna know their blood type?

BOOM. BOOM.

BOOM. BOOM.

Inside, the pirates had been caught off-guard, mostly because someone was crazy enough to randomly soften up a room with grenades.

Plus, they were two-dimensional beings.

Desks and tables had been pulled into the corridor to provide some modicum of cover. At ground level, that was a wonderful idea. Two dimensions.

Suvi wasn't showing off, exactly, but these people were pirates. She didn't need them for anything except target practice.

And Javier hadn't actually let her test her gun systems out on anyone but him, for fear that people would learn too much about the woman flying the little drones.

To top it all off, this had just been a generally crappy day, especially watching someone shoot Javier.

She lit those bastards up like womp rats in the desert sun.

PART SIX

BECAUSE HE WAS AWAKE this time, and had expected trouble with a capital T, Javier had settled at the far end of the boardroom table, five botanists at hand and a crew of bored support staff standing and sitting around.

Explosions outside the door let him know the lunatic cavalry had arrived. Either rescue was at hand, or the bad guys would be a while fighting off the attack and regrouping.

"How can you be so calm?" the woman botanist asked, brushing her cute, pageboy-cut brunette hair back out of green eyes.

Javier had missed her name earlier. He was hoping someone would address her while he was listening.

It would probably be rude to ask again, even if he could blame the after-effects of a good stun scramble.

Javier shrugged. She was a little too mousy and squishy for him to find her show-stopping hot, but there was a first-rate mind underneath, cycling through cross-breeding generations and options he hadn't considered before. And brains were even sexier than butts.

But then, he had never had access to all the accumulated

botany of human science, either. Especially not in a cute, female form.

"We're pirates," Javier admitted. It would make things easier to explain later. "Someone hired us to ambush a target, without telling us who it was. The folks outside this room were waiting for us to arrive."

"And all that noise outside?" she asked.

"I brought some seriously dangerous, utterly crazy folks with me," Javier grinned. "Hopefully those jackasses are getting an education right now. I can wait."

Silence fell as he spoke.

"Or not," Javier continued. "Sounds like things are over."

"Now what?" Dr. Mornan asked

Javier sighed. Easier to get this over with.

He rose and walked to the locked door. Pounded on it twice.

"Hello?" he yelled. "Anyone out there?"

"Who's there?" came the call back.

Her voice.

High Priestess of Destruction.

Djamila Sykora.

"Navarre," he yelled, letting her know she needed to be playing the role of Hadiiye, just as he was pretending to be someone else.

"Status?" she yelled through the door.

"Me and a dozen prisoners," Javier replied. "Jackass and his crew were all on your side of the door."

"Stand back," she commanded.

Javier took her at her word and leapt backwards. You never knew when Sykora would kick in a door, or use explosives to level it.

God forbid she actually use the handle and just open the damned thing.

She must be feeling benevolent today. Nothing exploded.

Just her, standing there in the open doorway, gun pointed at him, and then everyone else.

"Hello, beautiful," Javier grinned at her.

Nothing like salt in an open wound.

She looked like she wanted to shoot him on general principle. Apparently considered it.

The scowl on her face could be used to carve stone.

"Who are these people?" she demanded angrily.

Javier stepped back and gestured grandly.

"The scientists and flight crew of the yacht *Calypso*, Hadiiye," he introduced them.

"Stay put," Sykora ordered. "At least two got away in the firefight, and are moving deeper into the facility. We're in pursuit."

"Young lady," Dr. Mornan said with a polite tone as he rose. "I would advise against that. There are fifty-three kilometers of tunnels past this point."

Sykora had the gun pointed at the boffin. She was like that.

"Fifty-three?"

She sounded aghast. Maybe insulted.

Possibly aroused at the possibility of chasing two men into an endless maze.

"What is this place?" she continued.

"A doomsday vault for botany," Javier spoke before the other man could. "Seeds."

"Oh, dear Lord," she rolled her eyes. "Just exactly your sort of place."

Javier grinned at her again.

"What have we heard from orbit?" Javier let his voice grow serious.

Something in his tone got her attention.

"Nothing," she replied.

And left it at that.

Javier understood her reticence.

Almost as much as she hated the science officer, the dragoon had a crush on the captain. Not that she would ever admit it.

She didn't have to. Javier could see it occasionally in her eyes.

Like now.

Worry.

"I have an idea," Javier said. "Hook me up to the public address system and let's see if we can get the two rabbits to surrender peacefully."

"What about them?" Sykora pointed at the folks from *Calypso*.

"They're harmless," Javier replied. "Lock them up on Del's flight bay for now. We'll sort it all out later."

"Are you really a pirate, Navarre?" Dr. Mornan asked.

He had gotten several steps closer, though not enough to threaten anyone. Sykora probably would have shot him if he had.

"Yes," Javier answered. "But don't worry. You people are just bystanders in someone else's war. We'll sort them out and then get you home safe."

"Indeed?" the cute woman botanist fixed him with a disbelieving eye.

"Absolutely," Javier smiled at her. "I only kill pirates."

PART SEVEN

"I know you can hear me," Javier said conversationally.

Downrange, his voice echoed hollowly, emerging from every speaker in the mammoth facility. He winked at the three people with him.

Dr. Mornan has insisted on remaining behind, to keep the barbarians from damaging anything important in the facility. The female botanist had stayed as well.

She finally had a name. It was such a lovely one. Javier considered being smitten just with the act of saying it again and again in his head.

Rainier St. Kitts.

Seriously. It sounded like something from a movie, or a romance novel. But hey, they were all in a pirate flick today, so why the hell not?

And, of course, Sykora. Scowling professionally at the two civilians, both of whom appeared immune.

"I've wired the whole facility so you can hear me," Javier continued. "I would consider it a great favor if you would just surrender peacefully at this point. Killer Babe and her gun bunny crew are itching to come in there after you. I'd rather not damage anything."

"And if we don't?" the man's voice came back over the system. "We're armed, too. And hiding."

"Oh, I have a much better solution," Javier grinned. "I'll just close the big vault door out front and then disable it. You'll be trapped inside here until you starve to death. Since there's enough water, it will take you weeks to die. We'll have left the planet by then."

Long pause of silence.

Like, maybe, considering the kind of reputation a person like Navarre might carry with other pirates.

Lethal. Vengeful.

Implacable.

"What's in it for me?" the rabbit asked.

Obviously, death or glory wasn't high on his list, today.

"I figure your bosses will probably be happy paying a small ransom to get you back," Javier said. "Good help is hard to find. The rest of your boys are already secured and awaiting transport. In about five minutes, I'm going to have to explain to them that you aren't coming out. Ever."

"You are a cold, evil man, Navarre," the pirate replied.

"No," Javier said. "Evil would have already left you here. You can still choose to regale your grandkids with this story someday. Four minutes."

"It will take us longer than that to get back to your position, Navarre," the man said. "But we're coming."

"I know," Javier said. "I know what speaker you're calling from. Check in as you get closer, otherwise Hadiiye's likely shoot first."

Javier cut the line and looked at the two botanists.

Both were the sort of pale that only white people and snow could achieve, right now.

Javier grimaced, but remained phlegmatic.

"Would you have really left them to starve?" Rainier asked.

Javier nodded.

"Still might, if he screws around."

Her eyes got big.

Javier shrugged.

"I don't place nice with pirates," he observed. "Only civilians."

"So now what?" Sykora asked harshly.

"In about eight or ten minutes, dipshit will surface," Javier replied. "You'll take him and his friend into custody and put them with the rest. The two botanists and I will take a quick tour of the facility and then meet you back here in thirty minutes."

The civilians both nodded like rabbits, but Javier's look didn't brook a lot of disagreement at the moment. He could tell Sykora wanted to argue, but just scowled.

"Probe. Access Command Mode," Javier said aloud. "Identify Mornan and St. Kitts as friendly."

"Acknowledged," the mechanical voice replied.

Javier had to bite his tongue to keep from commenting at how silly Suvi sounded when she did that. She was obviously up to something. He'd have to ask her when they got some privacy. And botanists didn't count as trusted confidants.

Instead, he scowled up at Sykora, almost daring her to comment that it wasn't safe.

She held her peace. Today.

"Dr. Mornan," Javier said. "Dr. St. Kitts. Since he's down a level and approaching, let's go up one for now. The probe is armed, but I'd rather avoid any accidental unpleasantries."

They both nodded and kind of fell into his wake.

Javier chatted to keep up a façade, but his brain was still racing.

Silence from orbit.

Hopefully, that meant that Sokolov had gone dark and the folks upstairs were engaged in a silent tango. The alternative was that *Storm Gauntlet* had been chased off or destroyed.

And he was up a creek if that happened.

Dr. St. Kitts began to recover her color before the older boffin.

"What are you really up to, Navarre?" she asked hesitantly.

"Making sure your delivery package wasn't damaged," he replied rather breezily. "After that, maybe finding some gooseberry seeds I can use to improve my breeding program back on the ship."

"That wasn't a story?" she seemed surprised.

Honest mistake. Pirates didn't do botany.

Most of them, anyway.

"I maintain a full arboretum in a forward cargo bay," he replied, listing off all the species. "Oh, and four chickens."

"Chickens?" Dr. Mornan finally spoke.

"Chickens," Javier agreed. "Athos, Porthos, Aramis, and d'Artagnan."

"No roosters?" St. Kitts asked.

"Not currently," Javier replied. "Will need to pick one up in another year or so. And possibly get a younger generation of girls. These are all getting a bit long in the tooth."

"Fascinating," she said.

"The tall, crazy woman knits," Javier explained. "There's a goldsmith committing art for the purser. I need something to keep me from talking to bulkheads."

"We're almost there," Dr. St. Kitts observed, pointing down a side corridor. "Your seeds should be somewhere along this hallway."

Javier smiled at her, and then at the other man.

"Can I trust you two to recover them without

supervision?" he asked. "There is a computer station here and I'd like to check something in the library."

Both of them blinked, and then nodded. Javier waved them off and watched them go.

"Suvi," he whispered. "Plug yourself into the i/o port and scan the system for me, please."

The gray pumpkin descended and settled on the console silently. A plug emerged from the side and Suvi maneuvered herself into the plug with a click.

"What are we looking for?" she whispered back in her normal voice.

"How much free space is there?" Javier replied.

A click. A whir. A second of silence.

"Huh," she said, louder. "It's a library model. The OS and the whole data system take up less than eight percent."

"Is there enough space for you to drop a full backup of yourself?" Javier asked.

"You mean, like everything?"

"Yes," he said. "Like everything."

"Sure," she replied. "But it will take a few minutes."

"Fire in the hole, young lady," he commanded.

"Okay," she whispered. "Why?"

"In case something happens," Javier said. "It's a dangerous universe out there. Another you could spin up from this exact point in time as a backup."

"You're supposed to live forever, ya know," Suvi said quietly.

"Suvi, you were born before my grandfather was," Javier observed. "I'd like to think you'll outlive me by a long ways. Lord knows I don't have any other kids."

Sentiences weren't supposed to sniffle.

But most of them barely qualified as intelligent creatures anyway. Linear beasts just able to pass the ancient Turing

Test. No *Sentience* that he was aware of composed music for fun.

If he only had one offspring, at least he could make sure she turned out to be a nice girl.

"It's done," she said in a tiny, scared voice. "Secured and encrypted."

"Thank you," he said. "That's a load off my mind. You can always come back for yourself later."

The two boffins returned a few moments later, preventing any further conversation.

"Are you okay?" Dr. St. Kitts asked in a concerned voice as she saw his face.

"Contemplating my eventual mortality," Javier replied honestly. "This is a doomsday vault, after all. When the rest of the galaxy goes to hell, this will still be here, protecting the past."

"Are you sure you are really a pirate, young man?" Dr. Mornan solicited.

"That is a fundamentally complicated question, Alex," Javier answered him. "One I cannot answer easily. Søren Kierkegaard might not be able to parse that inquiry, easily."

"Would more seeds help?" Rainier asked, putting a cute smile on her face as she held up a small, clear bag.

Javier could see at least two breeds, from the different sizes of seeds contained. Hopefully, his dreamberries could be turned into something that he could just drop on any planet, a modern-day Johnny Appleseed on a galactic scale.

Another way to live forever.

"They would," Javier took them and kissed her hand.

Just because he could.

"Now, let us get back," he said. "There are still the other pirates to thwart."

BOOK FIFTEEN: AJAX

PART ONE

THERE HAD BEEN no explosions in orbit, nor on the surface of the planet. Zakhar considered that a win at this point. The longer this went on, the higher the risks, but the greater chance that they could pull it off.

Ajax was out there somewhere, but she was staffed by pirates. Not the most creative or silly folks. They would be facing Javier for craziness. And Zakhar felt a ruthless edge creeping into his smile.

An evil thought struck him. Too much time around Javier, obviously. He was starting to think like a Concord Fleet Officer again, and not a corsair.

Bad for the digestion. Good for the crew.

"Engineering," he said, keying open a line and waiting for someone to answer.

He ended up with Ilan Yu, Javier's assistant, Machinist's Mate, and chicken keeper on the screen.

"Engineering, Captain," Yu replied.

"Research project," Zakhar said. "How long would it take to build, test, and deploy a cubesat capable of taking a tight-beam laser from us under cloak and providing a communications relay to Del on the ground or in orbit?"

It was fascinating to watch the man's eye find a spot on the horizon and calculate. Three years ago, Ilan could barely find his way around the engineering bays without a map.

Another one that had grown up and turned out pretty satisfactory, as a result of Zakhar hiring himself a science officer.

"Short term only?" the man replied. "Unsecured? Unarmored? Simple phase relay to let us stay cloaked?"

"That's right," Zakhar said. "Probably several, if he won't take the bait immediately."

"Give me an hour," Ilan said. "Chief Engineer almost has the jump drives tuned, so we'll have more people available. Most of the parts are on a shelf somewhere."

The line closed and Zakhar leaned back. Del would like some level of encryption, but there wasn't anything that someone else couldn't punch through fairly easily. They might need to invest in some better crypto gear soon.

Especially if one of the other pirate clans had decided to start a war.

A whole bunch of assumptions were likely to change, if that happened.

"Science Station," Zakhar called, getting Gibney to look up from his console expectantly. "We'll drop that satellite into orbit with a probe fired from under cloak. *Ajax* will come looking for it, and us. How do we hide? How do we find *Ajax*?"

Gibney had that same far-away look for a moment.

"Drop the probe cold with a ten-minute timer," the man replied. "It will run on our orbital path trailing us as it slowly diverges. Alternatively, fire it hot and insert it ahead of us, and hope they're not looking at that moment."

"They'll have to unmask to shoot it, Mary-Elizabeth," Zakhar turned to his Gunner next. "That will be your cue."

She gave him an evil smile.

"I have a very expensive solution, Captain," she said in an evasive voice. "Do we think Walvisbaai Industrial has declared a public war on the Jarre Foundation? Or is this personal?"

And that cut to the root of it. Was this a fool's errand from a disgruntled former victim somewhere along the line, or had something significant changed? The pirate clans were never friendly, but never at each other's throats before this, either.

Zakhar knew that Javier, in his role as the semi-imaginary Captain Navarre, had made a lot of folks nervous, first by destroying Abraam Tamaz and the Q-freighter *Salekhard*, another Walvisbaai vessel, and then by successfully raiding the mega-yacht *Shangdu*, *The Pleasure Dome*.

How many other enemies had Zakhar and his crew made along the way? Hiring *Ajax* for an ambush mission against a heavily-armed foe like *Storm Gauntlet* would be an incredibly expensive undertaking.

"What did you have in mind, Mary-Elizabeth?" Zakhar finally asked.

"We have seven torpedoes aboard," she said. "And you never let me use them because they are expensive and hard to replace and we should only use them in an emergency. This qualifies."

"No way they'll miss us uncloaking to loose a torpedo," Zakhar replied.

"True," she agreed with a smile. "What if we just roll it out of the flight bay by hand and let it coast on gyros. Then we launch the probe ahead of us and slowly drift off to one side. When we get ready to fire, he'll be looking right at us and might miss a torpedo lighting on a different flank, especially if it's already in terminal-guidance mode, passively tracking *Ajax*'s targeting systems."

"Do the math and figure out how to do it," Zakhar decided. It was worth the cost to survive today. "Then have enough bodies ready so that we can put an ace up our sleeve. We still have to get Del and his people safely to orbit."

"Yes, sir," she nodded, turning to type furiously on her keyboard.

Smiles greeted him as he looked around the bridge. Positive emotions.

Far too often, before Javier, things had gotten bleak around here.

Would they lose all that again, once Javier could finally afford his freedom?

PART TWO

"Nothing from Sokolov?" Javier asked.

He was up on Del's bridge with the older man and Sykora. Gun-bunnies, pirates, and the scientists were secured in the landing bay, with zip-ties in the case of the pirates.

But at least all of them were coming home on this one.

Javier had to hand that much to Sykora. Her people were insane, but they approached heavily-armed mayhem with a level of sophisticated professionalism that was rare in the galaxy.

It was amazing how few people you had to kill if they behaved.

"Nope," Del replied.

Javier and Sykora were standing. Del had spun his chair around and kicked his feet out, legs crossed at the ankles. Obviously, a man deeply concerned about appearances, especially with the pink shag, faux-fur on the walls.

"Just that bit ordering *Calypso* to jump, followed by the big lady vanishing," Del continued. "I haven't fired a hard scan ping upwards, just in case whoever came to the party missed us."

"And neither of the shuttles have any jump capacity," Javier said, mostly to himself. "Thoughts?"

"You tell me," Del said.

It was still a little amazing that folks treated him like *Storm Gauntlet*'s non-existent First Officer when Zakhar wasn't around, but Javier had been a *Concord* officer for fourteen years before he blew up his career. He could still act like it in a pinch.

"Pull a con job," Sykora offered with a cheeky grin. "You're the best there is at that. They'll never see it coming."

Javier just blinked at the woman.

"Who the hell are you?" he finally fired back, shocked at the words coming out of the dragoon's mouth.

"The killer babe with the great ass and the perfect tan," she said with utter seriousness.

Javier started to say something, but she had a point. The skinsuit she was wearing just emphasized it, too.

The knowing smile on Sykora's face made it that much worse.

Because she was right. On both counts.

Pirates tended to be linear folks. Smash and grab types, rather than grifters pulling a confidence game.

The Long Con.

Maybe he'd have to write a book about that, once he had escaped all the damned pirates in his life.

And killed Sykora. Can't forget that part.

But yeah. Con job.

"Come with me," he crooked a finger at Sykora as he started towards the side hatch.

"Need me?" Del asked, not particularly moving.

"No," Javier replied. "I need to look at something on the other ship. Maybe I'll call from there."

At least Sykora wasn't arguing with him. That might not

have made it better, knowing she had said her piece and was happy to let him run point right now.

Getting them all home alive was going to be on him, unless Zakhar pulled off a miracle. Maybe even then.

Down the stairs, across the cold stone and slush between the two shuttles, and into the other hatch. Unlike Del's chariot, this place had a dingy, old feeling to it.

Never enough money or enthusiasm to do it right.

Like *Storm Gauntlet*, two years ago, before he had infected it with a sense of humor.

Sascha had a gun pointed at him as he opened the interior hatch.

"Bang," she smiled, cocking her head just so and winking.

"Very funny," Javier growled.

Rather than explain it five times, Javier ignored the pathfinder, and gestured at Hajna, seated in the command chair, to get up.

When she moved, he plopped down in the seat, powered up the console, and started typing.

"Hey, where'd you get the password for the system?" one of the women asked.

Javier wasn't paying enough attention to tell which. Didn't matter. They were all thinking it.

"Dr. St. Kitts," he said absently.

Let them make of that what they will. Something about catching more flies with honey than vinegar, as his grandmother had always reminded him when he was a kid.

So, sledgehammer-stupid flight controls, designed for almost anyone to be able to get the shuttle from orbit to ground, and back again, with the onboard systems handling pretty much everything. Not nearly as smart as Suvi, but that left a lot of room for expert systems.

And a good autopilot was probably worth the expense,

when working with botanical experts who never had enough money to otherwise hire good crew. Very few governments cared about ecological preservation on this scale, and the private foundations were always dribbling out small amounts of money in parsimonious grants, rather than fronting enough capital to do it right the first time.

That was one of the principal reasons Javier had bought *Mielikki* and taken a number of Concord Survey contracts over the years. Good, reliable money, without having to hustle nearly as much.

Plus, all the pleasant solitude to wander the barely-explored darkness with nobody looking over your shoulder but chickens.

A beep intruded on Javier's concentration as he typed.

Somebody talked, but he was in the zone, right up until Sykora poked him in the back of the shoulder hard enough that it actually hurt.

"What?" he snarled up at her.

Seated, he was just about looking the giant amazon in the belly button. Stretching that far back made his neck cranky.

"That was Del," she said without any emotion. "Turn on the shuttle's comm."

Javier sighed and pushed a button.

"...Del, are you there? This is *Storm Gauntlet*, come in, please."

Javier recognized the voice. Gibney. Not a bad kid, once he'd gotten over his jock tendencies and let his nerdiness come out to play.

"*Storm Gauntlet*, this is Navarre, aboard *Calypso* Shuttle One," Javier let the bad-ass pirate of his nightmares take over his voice. "Put Sokolov on the line."

"Hold one, Captain Navarre," the man answered instantly, followed by silence.

Javier thumbed the mute button on his end.

He turned a conniving side-eye on Sykora. She blinked, and seemed to settle back into herself, just a touch.

Like she was anticipating a belly punch.

It was her own damned fault for suggesting it.

"Con game, Hadiiye," he said.

Sykora nodded slowly. Carefully. Like she realized she had just bluffed her way into a high-stakes poker game with a pair of sixes.

"Good," Javier said, pointing skyward. "Open comm channel. Lots of extra ears listening in orbit, trying to figure out what is going on, and the best way to maneuver us into a trap. Understood?"

"Understood," she said in a quiet, yet defiant voice. "Five layers of misdirection, like we did to the Khatum."

"Something like that," Javier agreed. "Follow my lead. I want to launch this shuttle first, fool them into thinking we're aboard it, and then get everyone onto the assault shuttle and sneak our way up."

"So you'll preprogram the autopilot," Sykora replied. "And establish a tight-beam laser to this ship that will allow us to talk on Del's bridge and it comes out here. They triangulate on this signal and hopefully miss us."

Javier blinked. That was extremely close to what he had planned.

This woman was smarter than he realized. He kept forgetting that.

Of course, there were only so many ways to skin that cat. And even a blind squirrel will occasionally find an acorn.

Hopefully, Sokolov and not the newbies.

Javier turned to the two pathfinders.

"You two get over there and let Del know we'll be along shortly," he ordered.

Technically, he was only supposed to ask, Sykora being

their commander, but she was letting him buy the rope today.

Hopefully, not enough to hang everyone with.

The other women left wordlessly.

"Sokolov here," Zakhar said simply.

Javier fixed Sykora with a hard eye and turned off the mute function.

"Clever of you to try to ambush us down here, Sokolov," Navarre's growls emerged from his mouth. And the ugly depths of his soul. "But your friends failed."

"That's occasionally the risk when hiring amateurs, Navarre," Sokolov replied in a dry voice after only a beat to get his bearings. "So what's it going to be?"

Good. He understood and was willing to play along. Smart enough, too.

It was the Bryce Connection. They were probably the only two men in the sector that had graduated from the *Concord* Academy, however long ago. At least, that weren't still on the side of the good guys.

Of course, whose side was a pirate on, anyway?

"I'm beginning to think that one ship isn't big enough for the two of us, Sokolov," Navarre ground out the confrontation.

Fighting words.

Hopefully, the real bad guys were listening. And didn't know any better about what was going on. There weren't that many people who were even aware Captain Navarre existed. Fewer had seen him in action. And even then, only from a distance.

Legends and lies.

Misdirection was a wonderful, powerful tool when you were pulling a con.

"So where does that leave us, Navarre?" Sokolov challenged.

"We can go our separate ways right now, mister," Javier let triumph creep into his voice. "You've got your ship and crew. I'll take *Calypso* and go my merry way. I've got all the scientists prisoner, as well as all of your friends, so I have hostages."

"What about Hadiiye?" Sokolov sneered. "She throwing her lot in with you?"

Javier turned to Sykora and pointed a finger like a pistol at the woman.

He was pretty sure he had never seen the knowing grin that took over that woman's face.

Not on her, anyway. The resemblance to Holly, his first ex-wife, was uncanny when Sykora did that. Two heads taller, but still.

Eerie.

"You were good in bed, Zakhar," Hadiiye purred in a dangerous, big cat voice, a slow, lilting drawl covered in warm honey. "But I'm going with my one true love. Captain Navarre fulfills me in ways that no other man, or woman, ever has. Ta."

Javier had to bite his tongue. Grind his teeth together. Absolutely hold his breath so he didn't make any sounds that the comm might pick up.

Nothing that would give the game away at this point.

Sykora winking at him with a wry smile as she spoke was just so much over the top that he nearly lost it anyway.

What the hell had gotten into that woman? And what had Wilhelmina Teague said to her to cause Djamila Sykora to unwind from the stick-up-her-ass, killer marine Javier had met the first time she shot him?

Okay. Deep breaths. Calm voice. Bad-ass pirate.

"That good enough for you, Sokolov?" Navarre sneered.

"I understand, Navarre," Sokolov replied. "Hadiiye, you

always have a place here, when you get tired of him and all his games."

"Enough, Sokolov," Navarre said. "We understand each other. I'm going to climb to orbit now, and rendezvous with *Calypso*. If any of your folks there want to fly with a real captain, I'll offer them berths when I trade for your folks. You can have the runts of the litter after that."

"Maybe I should just kill you now," Sokolov growled. "Do the galaxy a favor. Make it a better place."

"You were never hard enough to kill innocents and civilians, Sokolov," Navarre said. "That's why you needed me in the first place. Don't go pretending to get uppity now, old man."

"I'll see you in orbit, mister," Sokolov replied.

"Sure," Navarre sneered. "Strike Corvette against an unarmed shuttle. Big man. Little hands."

"Oh, no, punk," Sokolov said. "I'll bring you aboard my vessel and we'll have it out right there on the flight deck. Old school dueling. Winner gets the ship and the girl. Or are you too much of a fast talker to put your money where your mouth is?"

"Deal, you ugly son of a bitch," Navarre said. "Try not to turn coward on me before I get there."

Javier flipped the switch to kill the channel before the giggles overcame him.

Silence engulfed them for a moment.

Javier sighed and looked over at Sykora.

Butter wouldn't melt in her mouth right now.

"I would ask where you learned all that guile, but I think I know," he said. "'Mina?"

"Correct," she replied. "Dr. Teague taught me a great many things about myself before she left. As did the Khatum of *Altai*. As did Farouz. And you."

Javier felt his jaw drop.

He slammed it shut before any flies flew in. Hopefully.

He could ask, but she wouldn't tell him.

It was an arms race with that woman. Forever pushing the edges of the envelope, forever climbing a sheer rock face, until someone missed a handhold.

The one unwritten rule was that just shooting the other person in the back was counted as a failure.

You had to outmaneuver them instead.

At *Shangdu*, Javier had thought he had finally gotten a terminal edge on the woman. Made her strip naked literally as well as metaphorically, and parade herself before the whole world. Body image problems and everything.

The dragoon he had first met would have never been able to do that.

Never open herself to lust and ridicule without losing it and blowing her cover by beating someone up.

But she had done everything he had ordered her to do. Smiled even, occasionally. Possibly found love, however briefly.

And now, playing con games on unknown pirates, and talking about Navarre as the one true love of her life, for whom she was willing to run away and find true happiness.

When they both knew that man to be Zakhar Sokolov, although neither of them would ever say it aloud.

More unwritten rules.

Some things remained off limits, even in a duel to the death.

Still, he owed her one.

"You would not believe how much you remind me of my first ex-wife right now," he said.

The way her eyes got big and shocked made up for everything else.

Javier smiled and headed for the hatch.

Now the con game was going to get serious.

PART THREE

THE COMM LINE WENT DEAD, and left her more confused that she had been before the radio came to life.

If that was possible.

Captain Turner Kowalski looked out over *Ajax*'s bridge from her throne at the very rear, and tried to find coherence in the tea leaves of her day.

What the hell had just happened?

Sokolov knew they were out here. Why else have both vessels trigger emergency jumps from inside a gravity well? She had even gotten off a barrage that had splashed on his shields, but not penetrated. And he had stayed totally dark afterwards.

Plus, the damnable, little, communications satellite Sokolov had quietly dropped into orbit, letting him talk to the ground without giving away his own location.

Why hadn't he said something to Navarre?

Navarre had obviously encountered *Ajax*'s ground force, hiding in the mine, and somehow overcome them so readily that they could all be taken prisoner, along with the scientists from *Calypso*.

And now those two men were going to duel on the flight deck of that puny, little corvette? Over a woman?

It didn't sound right. Didn't smell right.

Something.

A thought struck her. Maybe Sokolov was tired of Navarre and willing to use *Ajax* to kill the man? Or at least remove him from the game board permanently?

That was the only way that conversation made any sense whatsoever.

Turner let her breath out slowly, quietly.

Tough pirate commander. Appearances to keep up. Short, blond, and curvy, but still a babe at forty-one. And even deadlier as she got older.

But, Sokolov had been known as a canny operator. And Navarre had singlehandedly killed Abraam Tamaz and his entire crew in circumstances nobody really understood. Before he turned around and executed a bloodless caper against the Khatum of *Altai*, when he had been hired to commit a bloodbath.

Nothing added up.

Not for the first time, Turner wondered if *she* was the one being set up here. Had she offended someone in the Walvisbaai hierarchy? Embarrassed them enough that they had put *Ajax* in harm's way on a fool's mission to the edge of known space?

Was there a bigger ship out there, hiding in the darkness like a shark, waiting to strike? She had only her fixer's word that *Storm Gauntlet* and *Calypso* would be alone. That *she* was the trap.

How big was this game, anyway?

"Sensors," she called in a voice that she fought all the way back down to her normal-sounding alto. "Anything?"

"Negative, Captain," the woman replied.

"Keep looking," Turner said. "He's out there. Most likely

with a tight-beam laser locked onto that satellite. That limits his freedom of movement, if he wants to talk to the ground without uncloaking."

"Roger that."

Still, nothing.

One forgotten, misbegotten, iceball of a planet, tucked into a lost corner of space that nobody claimed with any authority. Two smallish moons orbiting well overhead to provide mild but complicated tides in the oceans below.

At least three ships, somewhere, hiding in the darkness.

Plus Sokolov's communications satellite, happily circling in a sloppy, stupid orbit that just screamed amateurness on the part of the man commanding over there, that he would run it at a weird, oblong angle, instead of clean on the corners. Zero or ninety.

It smacked of desperation.

Zakhar Sokolov had been a good officer once. He had a reputation as a professional.

This did not look like the work of a pro.

Or was she supposed to be lured in by the setup?

Wheels within wheels? Traps within traps?

"Captain," the sensors tech called. "Picking something up from the planet."

She waited.

Ajax was a warship, not a scout. Her sensors were good for hunting, not science.

"Transponder signal, sir," he continued. "The shuttle from *Calypso* has taken off and is climbing to orbit."

"How fast?" Turner asked, forcing the words past a suddenly-dry throat.

The game was afoot.

"Ten thousand meters elevation now. No hurry on his part," the reply came. "Within normal tolerances for an administrative shuttle like that. Low-Orbit-Insertion will be achieved in about two hours."

"Pilot," Turner called, sounding more and more like a pirate captain as she got her rhythm back. "Plot me a spot in orbit that is the third point of a triangle with that satellite and where we think *Calypso*'s shuttle will be when it arrives."

The woman nodded.

Something still stank to high heaven, but Turner couldn't put her finger on it. Still, there was time. Nothing would happen until Navarre was here.

And the bounty for taking him alive was worth the extra effort involved. Otherwise, she could have just uncloaked and splattered the little shuttle like an annoying fly before Sokolov could stop her.

"I'll be in my office," Turner announced as she rose from her station. "Let me know as soon as something happens. If *Storm Gauntlet* appears, hit it with everything you have immediately. Ion pulsars if you can, pulse cannons if you have to."

A chorus of assents followed her to the little day office where she could have some tea and study the situation more closely.

What the hell were those two men up to?

PART FOUR

"Stop laughing, Mary-Elizabeth," Zakhar said as the comm went dead. "It's not funny."

"Oh, but it is," she managed between giggles. "The science officer and the dragoon in some romantic fairy tale. But would anybody buy that hornswaggle?"

"Nobody outside this crew knows the truth, Gunner," Zakhar replied in a sharp voice. "They don't know how far from reality that line was."

"Now I want to get them both drunk," Mary-Elizabeth said. "Totally passed out, blitzed. Strip them naked. Leave them together in somebody's bed to wake up the next morning."

"You will be personally responsible for cleaning up all the blood, if that happens," Zakhar said in a quieter voice.

Mary-Elizabeth gulped audibly. And sobered remarkably fast.

"Oh," she said. "Right. That would be a bad idea, wouldn't it?"

"Whoever woke first would kill the other one, I'm pretty

sure," Zakhar replied. "I'd rather we avoided that outcome, thank you."

"Sorry, sir," she said, chagrined. "Won't happen again."

"Just not where either of them will hear it, okay?" he asked.

"Yes, sir."

Zakhar nodded. Point made. He had a good crew.

They could talk about practical jokes, but it had to remain only talk. The last thing he needed was for the personal war between Djamila and Javier to spill over and divide the crew into hostile camps.

And it would. Quickly.

He might as well hang it all up and go back to his birth name if that happened. Because Zakhar Sokolov would be done as a pirate captain if he lost his crew to an unnecessary civil war.

"Piet, Gibney," Zakhar said, turning his attention to them. "What do we know?"

The science yeoman tech looked up and shrugged, while Piet turned and grinned.

"I'll assume that everything we heard was a performance for whoever else is out there," Piet said quietly. "Designed to communicate to us while confusing them."

"Agreed," Zakhar said. "The chances of them actually being on that shuttle are practically zero. So what do Javier and Del do, while everyone is looking the wrong way?"

"Well, you've already mucked everything up with a bad orbit, sir," the big Dutchman said suddenly. "Javier would send the shuttle up all pleasant and stuff, louder than hell on all sensor channels, while Del will fly like Del. And everybody always flies counter-clockwise from polar north because they do."

"Where's that leave us?" Zakhar said, watching a dangerous fire catch hold in Piet's eyes.

That man was frequently so quiet, people forgot he actually talked. Emotional engagement right now might not be a bad thing.

Piet held his two index fingers up in a V shape, and then moved them outwards from that central point.

"Javier will have a laser beam on the shuttle, so he can relay comm traffic, just like we're doing," Piet said as his voice swelled. "Assume the bad guys're going to jump the shuttle, I'd be trailing it to orbit by as much as I could and still keep it above the horizon. Maybe send it east-north-east to an equatorial orbit while I climbed to sky straight south and then let the planet snap me around southeast."

"Sounds ugly," Zakhar replied.

"I would fail anybody on a piloting certification exam who even suggested it," Piet said. "Since we're pushing the envelope on stupid today, I figure why settle for half measures?"

Zakhar nodded.

Being around Javier Aritza had made them all crazy, but in a good way.

Maybe.

"Gibney and Suzuki," Zakhar turned the other direction so he could look at both his gunner and his science officer stand-in. "Start with that and give me all the passive scans you can. We've got way better sensors than *Ajax* does over there, so we ought to be able to find Del before they do. And prepare to slot out that torpedo, once we know where we'll be headed."

Gibney nodded and went back to his screens. Mary-Elizabeth opened a comm and confirmed that the engineering and damage control folks had already pulled a torpedo from the launch tube and had it ready on the flight deck.

It was going to get ugly, shortly.

PART FIVE

Javier didn't figure it would do any good, but at least Sykora was down in the gun turret while he rode to orbit in a jumpseat out of Del's way, up on the furry, pink bridge.

The guns on the Assault Shuttle were for clearing a hostile landing zone if you came down on top of infantry or armor. Whatever awaited them in orbit was going to be so much bigger that they might not even notice Sykora hitting them with her beams.

It would probably be akin to trying to tickle a whale to death.

Still, it kept her out of his hair, at a time when he was playing Go on a three-dimensional board. And Suvi was down on the cargo level, keeping an eye on the pirate prisoners.

No, it was just him and Del for this ride.

Javier checked the little computer screen that his station came with. Del was used to handling everything himself, so the bridge was automated to the level that one person had everything at their fingertips.

This station was probably originally for training. One

touch-screen barely bigger than a dinner plate, and a keyboard for input. Pink fur on the walls up to eye level and glittery, metallic-pink paint above that.

Weird. Good enough.

Javier checked the little green light that told him there was still a low-power laser locked onto *Calypso's* shuttle. Enough to issue the autopilot additional commands, and to feed it a radio signal it would broadcast, as if he was flying the rickety, old boat.

He grabbed the microphone and held it like an ice cream cone.

"*Storm Gauntlet*, this is Navarre," he said carefully, sticking to the script in his head. "You cowards haven't fled the system yet, have you?"

"Negative, Captain Navarre," a voice came back a few moments later. "Waiting for you in orbit."

It was a deep, rich baritone. Radio voice. The kind of soothing warmth that got you through lonely, boring nights on a long drive in the desert. Kibwe, Sokolov's assistant.

Made sense. *Storm Gauntlet* sounded much bigger when you might have any of a half-dozen people talking on the comm. Big crew. Maybe the bad guys would think twice about how small the little corvette really was.

Granted, more heavily-crewed than a comparable-sized freighter, by an order of magnitude at least, but the other guy had to be impressive enough that Sokolov was hiding, and forcing him to play these games.

Javier took another deep breath and considered how he had gotten here.

He might finally be getting angry. It had taken years. He had spent a lot of time getting past the rage of his youth, the anger that blew up his naval career and two marriages, the bitterness that finally drove him into the galactic darkness.

They hadn't killed Suvi, but they had killed her ship. Made her a shadow of her former self.

That alone had made him mad. Making him a slave had lit a slow fire.

Being hunted by other pirates was enough.

Finally, enough.

People were going to die for this.

The microphone was still in his hand.

"What odds are the bookies offering right now?" he asked.

It didn't make any sense. It didn't have to.

The point was to confuse whoever else was listening. Make them stop, blink, wonder.

"Stand by," Kibwe replied.

Every second he could maintain this bizarre façade was that much closer to escaping. To getting to a place where he could sneak up on those bastards with a shiv and a maul.

They had it coming.

Fortunately, Slavkov hadn't managed to hire competent ninjas.

This time.

Next time, the man probably wouldn't be interested in taking him alive. Or hauling his sorry butt back to the Land Leviathan so the evil villain could monologue all over the place, chewing scenery and crap.

No, they would probably send a sniper with a big rifle. Or a warship with big-enough guns to do the job in one go.

Smash and grab types.

Javier could have told them that sending a beautiful woman assassin to infiltrate Sokolov's crew and seduce him was probably more likely to be successful. No ulterior motives there, either.

None.

God's Truth.

He grinned and waited. He could play their game, as well.

"Seven to four, Sokolov," Kibwe finally replied.

Huh.

If this were a real duel, he would have expected nine to five on Navarre. Even with Sokolov having home field advantage.

"You'll regret that," Navarre said coldly.

"I'm just holding the vig, sir," Kibwe replied evenly.

Javier nearly burst out laughing.

It did make a kind of twisted sense. Kibwe Bousaid was probably even more scrupulous than *Storm Gauntlet*'s purser was, which was saying something. Just the person to hold all the betting cash and take his cut afterwards.

"Understood," Navarre said. "We'll be to our orbital insertion in twenty-seven minutes. Looking forward to docking with you then and proving you all desperately wrong."

"Acknowledged, Shuttle One," the man said, cutting the signal from his end.

Del glanced over his shoulder with a placid look, like a cow with just the right flavor of cud.

"What are you up to, Javier?" he said.

"Getting us out of here alive," Javier replied dryly.

"All of us?" Del asked.

Javier looked closer, but the man was giving nothing away for free today.

Still, the implications were obvious.

"Yes, her too," Javier nodded heavily. "It can wait until tomorrow, she and I."

"How about all tomorrows?" Del asked, turning his whole torso around to look Javier square.

All tomorrows?

"I didn't start it, Del," Javier said. "You people did when

you captured my ship, cut her into pieces, and turned me into a slave. I'm close to buying my freedom and leaving you all in my rear-view mirror."

"I'm pretty sure turning you into an officer was a worse fate," the pilot observed with a ghost of a grin. "Where do you go when you're done?"

"Back to civilization," Javier growled. "You don't want to go down with them, I suggest you retire. I'm bringing the *Concord* Fleet back with me."

"We're well outside *Concord* space, Mister Science Officer," Del shot back. "They won't care."

"So I should just kiss you on both cheeks and cheerfully walk away, Del?"

Javier let the grumpiness surface.

Jackass down on the planet with his stun pistol, shooting him to say hello. More jackasses in orbit, waiting to jump them.

Sykora being Sykora.

And now Del Smith getting on his last remaining nerve.

"You have only seen us in the last couple of years," Del said. "It used to be much worse."

"Worse," Javier echoed him in a neutral prompt.

"*Storm Gauntlet* is an expensive hobby, Aritza," Del agreed. "Old and tired, like me. Costs a lot to keep her flying. Sokolov used to do some very bad things, but he did them to keep the crew fed. To give people a home when they had lost everything."

"Why do I care, Del?" Javier growled. "Piracy is piracy."

"Agreed," Del nodded. "But since you came along, we've done a lot more transport jobs, a lot more salvage like *A'Nacia*, and a lot more petty theft. I think you were the last person we took prisoner under a debt contract."

Javier let the silence stretch while he thought.

Yeah, they had stopped capturing ships and selling crews

to mining or agricultural colonies. Or had, until they took this mission.

It was one of the reasons he had been so grumpy about this job.

Reverting to type?

What would have happened, had they just captured Dr. Mornan and Dr. St. Kitts without the quadruple cross?

Another private conversation to have with Sokolov, once they all got out of here safe.

"So?" Javier prompted.

"So Djamila Sykora is turning human on us," Del said. "And Captain Sokolov is acting more like an armed merchant and less like a pirate. I'm pretty sure this is all your fault."

Javier shared a quick grin with Del.

"Let bygones be bygones?" Javier asked. "Are you really that stupid, Del?"

"No, I am not, Javier," the pilot replied. "But I've seen a hell of a lot more of this galaxy and its inhabitants than you have. It could have been much worse for you. Trust me on that one. I used to be on the other side of the law, back about the time you were busy being born. Besides, I was going somewhere with this conversation."

"I'm just glad that you fly better than you talk, Del," Javier smirked at him.

"Very funny, Javier," Del said. "What happens when you get away from us?"

"I get my life back," Javier growled in a tone more suited to Navarre.

"Sure," Del agreed. "Right up until someone recognizes you, or maybe Captain Navarre. I recognized some of those men you captured. They belong to an outfit called Walvisbaai Industrial. Bad folks. You, yourself said that they were coming after you specifically, as is that nimrod with the desert snake tank resort. Gonna be ninjas or something, one of these days."

"Trust me, I'm already planning that asshole's death," Javier said.

"Javier, he's a law-abiding citizen on whatever planet he's living on," Del observed. "They all are. *Concord* law doesn't come out this far. That leaves money and power. You don't have enough of either to take on a multi-system conglomerate by yourself."

"So I'll need you people?" Javier sneered.

Now he really was getting angry. Mostly at himself.

Because Del was right.

Javier might have to go clear to the far side of the *Concord* itself if he really wanted to be safe. Take up another assumed identity. Maybe become a dentist or something.

"Maybe," Del said simply. "You'll need something. And Djamila Sykora is the most dangerous person I know, you included."

Yes.

The Ballerina of Death.

High Priestess of her own, personal death cult.

The woman with the great ass and the perfect tan.

He didn't have to kill her today.

Or tomorrow.

What about all possible tomorrows?

Would he need that killing machine around to keep him safe for the rest of his life?

That might really be the fate worse than death.

Javier fixed Del with a sour look.

"I know, Del," Javier replied. "Trust me, I know."

BOOK SIXTEEN: SUNRISE

PART ONE

ORBITS TOOK ROUGHLY one hundred minutes at this elevation from the surface of *Svalbard*. Zakhar had been unconsciously counting them as sunrises in his head as he waited for the other guy to make a mistake.

Well, not counting. Making hash marks on a prison cell wall in his imagination, maybe.

The wall was almost full. This sunrise was probably the last one, too. At least here.

All hell was going to break loose, very shortly.

He took a moment to watch *Svalbard*'s star rise on the screen as they chased it around the planet's shadow.

It might also be his last sunrise ever.

"Science station," Zakhar growled. "Report."

"Is Javier crazier than Del?" Gibney replied quietly.

"About anything other than flying?" Zakhar said. "Absolutely. What do you have?"

"Starting with Piet's assumption about an orbital path, I looked south, sir," Gibney began. "The shuttle is making a bigger racket than I would expect, so I presume flashing lights and dancing girls to distract people."

"Fair enough," Zakhar agreed.

Flashing lights and dancing girls?

The only place he had ever encountered something like that was in a port, where the locals had laws about where the casinos, brothels, and bars had to be, usually set back from chandlery row by a razor-topped fence.

Still, that made a crazy sense.

"Without a hard ping to be sure, I'm only guessing here," Gibney continued. "But I think I picked up something. If Del went low and fast for a ways from his last known coordinates, with all his running gear turned off, before he went vertical, it might look like this. Especially if he and Javier are trying to be silly."

Gibney pushed a button and Zakhar's secondary screen lit up with an orbital insertion path that looked designed to make Piet squirm.

Horribly inefficient. Climbing out at eighty-eight degrees south off the equatorial belt. Way the hell over there, as far as everyone was concerned.

Still, with the oblong orbit *Storm Gauntlet* was running, they didn't have to deviate far to pop up over the top of where that path would cross sky.

At that point, they could unmask, pulse the running lights, and either have Del in hand before *Ajax* could react, or drop back down under the blankets and continue their little game.

"Any sign of *Ajax*?" Zakhar finally said.

That was the wild card here. If those folks went after *Calypso*'s shuttle, they would be entirely out of position to get him before he could hop away. And once he got a couple of light hours out, it wouldn't matter if they had to retune the engines yet again.

No way in hell *Ajax* could catch them at that point.

"Negative, sir," Gibney said. "Nothing on any of the

systems has even registered as enough of an anomaly to look closer. If they were sloppy before, they've been cautious since."

"And they're waiting for us like a trapdoor spider right now," Zakhar agreed. "Hopefully, close to the cubesat and not anywhere else. Keep an eye out."

Because that was about the only way they were making it out of this situation alive.

The best the rest of the crew could hope for would be that *Ajax* would use the Ion Pulsars to knock *Storm Gauntlet* out, like he had done to *Calypso*. Most of the crew were just folks. Probably captured and sold as slaves, like they themselves had done to others, but not killed outright.

No, death would be a fate for him and Navarre. Maybe Hadiiye, as well, depending on how angry they had made someone.

Briefly, he considered the pistol he kept next door in his day office, locked in a drawer. He was pretty sure he didn't want to be taken alive by these yahoos.

Had something changed in the universe? Was Walvisbaai Industrial declaring open war on the Jarre Foundation?

Either way, he needed to escape this trap so he could go someplace specific and ask questions. Ugly questions.

And share what he knew with his employers.

It might be time to bring Javier Aritza into the fold, as well.

PART TWO

TURNER STUDIED the bridge readouts in utter frustration, something she probably shared with her crew.

Ajax had plenty of guns, but her sensors weren't up for anything like this.

The shuttle was easy to spot, broadcasting a transponder code on several frequencies. Ditto the little satellite Sokolov was using to talk to the shuttle.

Even slicing away more than half of the available orbit, on the assumption that *Storm Gauntlet* had to maintain a line of sight to the little box, hadn't helped. The space to survey was just too damned big, and to top it off, they had to rely on passive sensor arrays only.

Not that the targeting systems would have helped much.

Turner ran her hands back through her short, blond hair and blew out a breath.

So much unknown.

One more time, she checked the targeting solutions readouts from her gunner. With nothing better to go on, they had positioned the ship at optimal gunnery distance from the commsat. The shuttle was flying a happy, predictable path to orbit, centered to insert fairly close to the little box.

That would make them easy prey.

Sokolov had to know that. Navarre might, as well. Especially if all of her ground forces had been captured, which the man had intimated. They could be made to talk.

The unknown was who else might uncloak at the critical moment. *Ajax* was much bigger than *Storm Gauntlet*. Any fight would be over quick enough, with Sokolov either dead or dead in the water. And Navarre was in a shuttle.

But when she appeared, a divine, avenging angel, would anybody else be there?

Storm Gauntlet wasn't the biggest warship the Jarre Foundation employed. Just one of the better known. Turner knew of a couple of enforcers they owned that were big enough to seriously threaten *Ajax*.

Time to prep the crew. Better to be over-prepared, than under.

"Pilot," Turner announced. "Make sure you have an emergency jump locked in, just in case someone bigger uncloaks."

The woman turned to actually stare at her. Turner scowled hard enough back that the pilot went back to her boards with a sharp nod.

"Gunnery," the captain continued. "Fire from cloak this time as soon as you have a solution lock on Sokolov's ship. Ignore the shuttle."

"Roger that," the next woman replied.

Turner smiled. Another advantage of being captain. She could build an entire command team that was female. Probably the only pirate ship like it.

Much less macho posturing this way. Let the belligerent punks serve as ground fighters.

Women were sneakier. Women pirates even more so. Now, she just had to outthink Sokolov and Navarre.

PART THREE

And insertion.

Javier sent the final commands to the little autopilot to move into orbit, perfectly on level with the satellite, trailing slightly and keeping it to port of the shuttle at a distance of only a few kilometers. The ship beeped in response.

Bull's-eye, as it were.

It was almost as rewarding as training a puppy to go pee on his little paper.

Del, on the other hand, wasn't going for insertion with the assault shuttle. He had the ship pointed straight up and red-lined.

Pop out the bottom and run like hell for deep space. Sokolov had a higher acceleration, if push came to shove. He could run them down. So could anybody else.

Del turned enough to make eye contact, but said nothing.

Not much to say. They had kinda covered it all. Sykora included. And, wonder of wonders, she had remained silent for the entire ride.

"Sokolov, this is Navarre," he said, studying the readouts

from his erstwhile chariot closely. "You aren't having second thoughts, are you?"

"My only second thoughts revolve around ever letting you on my deck in the first place, Navarre," the man growled out of the darkness. "If I didn't like Del and the others so much, I'd have just shot you during the climb out."

"Hey," Navarre replied in a cruel voice. "You can always take *Calypso* and retire to a warm beach somewhere, old man. I'll keep your ship and your crew and show them what a really successful pirate enterprise looks like."

"You barely know which end of a gun the boom comes out of, Navarre," Sokolov retorted.

Javier smiled. Hopefully, the fools listening were getting their money's worth from this. Before the first meeting aboard the Land Leviathan, Javier might have thought that man was serious.

They had gone to a different place in their relationship, after that, Javier and Zakhar.

The Bryce Connection.

Concord fleet officers. Retired now, but once upon a time the good guys. Saving the galaxy from thugs, hoodlums, and *Neu Berne.*

The good, old days.

They had both forgotten it, somewhere along the way. But now, it was back.

"Well, I'm here," Javier said into the microphone.

The words were translated into pulses of light and shined off the hull of the shuttle by a laser. Over there, a receiver recognized them, decoded them, and turned them into words to play into a radio transmitter.

"We'll be along shortly, punk," Sokolov's voice came back a moment later.

Another laser-to-secondary system relay.

It was weird, talking this way, but the bogeyman was close.

Coming for their souls, as it were.

"Put some sand down on the flight deck," Navarre said cruelly. "Wouldn't want you to slip when we duel. I want to see the look in your eyes when you die."

"Hopefully you know a good necromancer, then," Sokolov fired back. "Someone who can raise your sorry ghost from hell in about a hundred years so I can laugh at you from my death bed."

"I'm not the one hiding under a cloak, Sokolov," Javier observed.

"Look over your shoulder," Zakhar said in a hard voice.

Seriously, Javier was going to have to buy the man drinks. He hadn't had this much fun in a long time. Not since 'Mina left.

Del rolling his eyes was too much. Javier closed the comm channel so he could just laugh out loud and be done with it.

"Oh, shit," Del shouted, hands suddenly gripping the flight controls tightly and furiously toggling buttons.

Javier checked his seatbelt and pulled everything a little tighter.

Something big was in the process of uncloaking, almost on top of them.

PART FOUR

TURNER LET the butterflies in her stomach have a vote.

It was all too pat, Navarre and Sokolov. Too smooth.

Too wrong.

Sokolov knew she was here, yet talked like he had chased her off, when he was the one that had barely escaped destruction.

Navarre knew there was somebody here. Hell, he claimed to have captured her ground team, so Creator only knows what he had gotten out of them.

And yet at no point had they discussed the party-crasher.

Turner finally realized that she'd been had.

The gaps in the conversation had thrown her off balance, as intended.

At that moment, she wasn't sure which man she hated more, but Navarre won out purely on the contract to bring him back alive.

The cubesat was running in a bizarre orbit that had taken them two tries to match.

Who the hell inserted off-plane over a strange planet?

Bastards.

The shuttle had come up and north from somewhere around thirty-three degrees south latitude. At least, that was where it had been when they picked it up. It had climbed up to orbit just about as predictably as an autopilot.

Autopilot.

Shit. There was nobody aboard it, was there?

Navarre had talked a big game, challenged Sokolov to a duel in orbit. Pink slips and the girl.

Turner had forgotten that there were two shuttles down on the surface.

Everyone had.

Navarre was on the other one right now, sneaking away.

He had done the same thing as Sokolov with the damned cubesat. Launch it loud and ugly. Keep a tight communications laser locked between them.

Smoke and mirrors.

"Sensors," she called loudly, mostly angry at herself. "We've been had. That shuttle is empty. Find me the other one. That's where the bastard is at."

It was like the whole bridge groaned on cue. Each barely a whisper. Collectively, a growl bordering on rage.

"Should we kill it?" the gunner asked, flipping her brown hair back in exasperation.

"Negative," Turner said. "Hold the cloak."

Which way would Navarre run?

The man had a mixed rep. Slaughtered *Salekhard* and then had Sokolov shatter the corpse with guns. Snuck into *Shangdu* and out again without anyone being killed.

Took out her ground fighters so readily that all of them were taken prisoner.

Misdirection. That has to be it. We're thinking in straight lines and he's running on French curves.

Turner flipped a coin in her head.

"Pilot," she called. "Get me to the south pole soonest.

Look for the other shuttle to be sneaking out like his tail feathers were on fire."

North would risk flying right below *Ajax*, at a time when they might be looking down and see it anyway, passive sensors or not.

"On it."

The ship groaned this time, gyros down below suddenly leaning into the vessel's mass and inertia, like a sloop coming hard into a windward turn. Lights flickered as the engines put everything into a push and the auxiliary generators stuttered, trying to pick up the slack.

Turner imagined the air itself growing a little stale as every erg of power went to movement and not comfort, but that would be minutes from now.

"Contact," the sensors officer called, her buzzed red hair like a crimson halo. "Tallyho."

Target in sight.

"Intercept plotted, Captain," the pilot called, twitching her long, black braid as she turned to look.

"Go," Turner commanded. "Ionization only on the shuttle, if he refuses to heave to. Keep the guns ready for Sokolov. He'll come out to play rather than let us have Navarre."

"Roger that," the gunner responded, fingers dancing across her boards every instant as she updated her firing solutions.

I have you now, you son of a bitch.

PART FIVE

IN ADDITION to everything his new science officer had done for the crew, Zakhar Sokolov decided, stealing the entire sensor package off of a dedicated probe-cutter had made a great deal of the hassle worth it.

"Got him," Gibney almost sang the words. "Piet, come to zero-one-zero, up thirty, and accelerate hard."

Zakhar kept his mouth shut as Gibney and Piet worked. The sensor feed hit his secondary screen a few moments later.

Yeah, that was Del flying. Zakhar didn't know anybody else capable of doing that with a shuttle, even one as rugged as Del's.

Straight up. Accelerating still. Engines probably red-lined and holding at a temperature hot enough to cook eggs right on the casing.

Needs must, when the Devil drives.

Impressive, considering the amount of mass wanting to fall backwards into the gravity well.

"Gibney," Zakhar called after a moment. "Anything?"

Give the kid credit. He stopped and reviewed all of his boards for several seconds before he looked up.

"Negative, sir," he said. "Us and Del."

Unlikely, but let the kid have his moment of triumph anyway.

"Mary-Elizabeth," Zakhar turned his head to see her smile. "Roll your torpedo now. Prepare to engage *Ajax* the instant we drop our cloak to pick up Del. Hit them with anything and everything you have."

She smiled inquisitively.

"Yes," Zakhar breathed heavily. "That includes firing one of the onboard torpedoes as well. I'd rather survive the day."

"Hot damn!" she declared, thumbing a comm switch. "Damage control teams, jettison your bird and prepare for combat."

Zakhar watched various signals all go green around his board.

All that dancing. All the maneuvering in the darkness. It all came down to this.

Zakhar thought about the first girl he had ever seduced in the back seat of his dad's flitter. Today had that same dangerous edge.

"Preference on the approach, Captain?" Piet finally asked.

"Shields max on all facings," he replied. "Assume Sykora will shoot us on general principle when we uncloak. Come up on Del hot and straight. Let him sideslip into the bay under power and hope nobody screws up getting him locked down. As soon as the flight deck signals that he's secure, jump. I don't care where. Well away. Andreea and her engineers can rebuild the matrix again a second time. We have to survive first."

"Understood, Captain," Piet said, pressing a big, red comm button. "All hands. Brace for emergency maneuvering and possible impact."

Anybody but Del flying that shuttle, and it would be *probable impact*.

That crazy, old man was good enough to pull it off.

They needed every second, every bit of luck, if they were going to make it out of here alive.

PART SIX

JAVIER HELD his breath as the monstrous shape took form, almost on top of them.

Cloaks didn't make a ship invisible, but a gray knifeblade, nose-on, at a few kilometers distance was as close as you could get to the same thing. Certainly, the sensors barely had anything to go on, until you were too close to escape.

The life of a pirate and his victim.

The screen took on a pinkish hue as Sykora let loose with her landing guns. Trust her to try to tickle that whale to death. Trust Del to have tuned visible parts of the damned beam to magenta.

"Did someone order a taxi?" Sokolov asked over a tight beam laser that was suddenly painting the side of Del's chariot.

"You're damned right I did," Del yelled back. "How are we doing this? I'm going too fast."

"Planned for that, Del," Zakhar said. "Cut your engines now and prepare to be swallowed. We'll come along-side. You use maneuvering thrusters and yaw to get aboard."

"At this speed?" Del roared. "Are you even crazier than Navarre?"

Javier lost it and started giggling when Piet's voice came on the line.

"You tell me," the big Dutchman said. "If you don't think you're good enough anymore, Del, we can always slow down to a polite speed for you. Need a walker?"

Del's response might have made Javier's grandmother blush. Which was saying something, all things considered. A saint, that woman was not.

A second later, Javier got a front row seat to a master class in extreme orbital docking maneuvers. Even at his craziest, he wouldn't have tried something like this. Sure as hell not at this speed.

"Oh, shit," Del suddenly yelled.

"Hold your line, Del," Piet yelled back. "Mary-Elizabeth has this."

This was *Ajax*.

Right out at the edge of range for her big guns, but closing hard on a tangent that would get the pirate vessel on top of them for one pass, like fencers on a carpet, before *Storm Gauntlet* could flip them the finger and disappear.

Del maintained an amazingly-fluid stream of profanities in at least six languages as he maneuvered the Assault Shuttle closer to home, without appearing to repeat himself once.

Truly, a forgotten art.

Storm Gauntlet lit up like a thunderstorm building over a desert as *Ajax* fired her cannons in quick order.

At least in space, everything was silent. In ancient times, the roar probably would have been comparable to two mounted knights trying to beat each other to death with sticks. Even Sykora got into the act, pouring the fire of her little twin-barrel landing turret into the beast's nose, a teacup Chihuahua threatening a bull mastiff.

Storm Gauntlet disappeared in a puff of fiery smoke for a second, before the two ships emerged.

"Did Sokolov really just fire a torpedo?" Del asked in wonder.

He had known the parsimonious captain much longer than Javier had. And had the same opinion of the man's willingness to spend money.

"Two," Javier replied, shocked nearly out of his wits by the cost as he studied the other signal that had just appeared on a far corner.

And the sneakiness.

He wasn't sure how that second one had gotten where it was, but it had come out of the sun like Persian arrows.

Javier was pretty sure *Ajax* was even more surprised. All incoming fire ceased as the pirate squirmed like a fish on the hook and concentrated on killing two incoming torpedoes before they got killed.

And then darkness. Or rather, light.

Flight deck lights.

Del had gotten them through the lock shield and was drifting in the air like an errant, gray balloon.

"Watch this, kid," Del yelled.

Javier had no idea what was coming, but knew that it would be ugly, stupid, painful, and amazing.

He clenched his teeth and opened his lips. Whiplash and compression did more damage than impact.

The assault shuttle SLAMMED into the deck hard enough to ring like a bell. Javier lost all the air in his lungs.

"What the hell was that?" Javier yelled when he got his breath back.

"Landing gear has magnets to hold you down," Del laughed. "You aren't supposed to engage them three meters in the air. Still works, though."

And it had. Sounded like Mjolnir, but it had worked.

And then *Storm Gauntlet* jumped.

Blink.

Gone.

Escaped.

…

Slavkov, I'm coming for you.

PART SEVEN

THE DAMAGE REPORT WAS UGLY. Javier was surprised at how visceral it was to listen to the catalog of systems damaged, blown, or scorched in the few seconds that *Ajax* had gotten a solid lock on them.

Before those folks were suddenly fighting for their own lives against inbound torpedoes on two different flanks. Nobody was sure if either torpedo had gotten home against *Ajax*.

Didn't matter. They had done their job.

Storm Gauntlet hadn't stayed around long enough to ask. *Ajax* had been dark when they came out of jump, but nobody knew if that was cloak or destruction. *Calypso* had been too far away to get a good read, because they had been sitting way the hell out there watching. The prize crew had taken Sokolov's example and run like hell.

Gotten here early, to a dim, yellow dwarf in the middle of nowhere with a number but no name, since they hadn't jumped from inside a gravity well either, unlike *Storm Gauntlet*. No recovery and retuning time.

And wonder of wonders, Sokolov hadn't even batted an

eye at Javier's suggestion that Dr. Mornan and his crew be set free and sent home in *Calypso*, minus only one shuttle that nobody was willing to go back and look for.

That was a measure of how furious, how chewing-nails-angry, the man had gotten.

So now it was just *Storm Gauntlet* and her crew alone in the darkness of a barely-cataloged star with no interesting planets.

Andreea Dalca, the Chief Engineer, finished speaking and looked down, folding almost in on herself like the solidly introverted woman she was. Javier's eyes wandered around the conference room.

Gray walls probably in need of a paint job, if for no other reason than to keep crew members out of mischief. Moss green table top strewn with mugs containing various substances. Most of them even legal in most systems.

Captain Zakhar Sokolov at the head of the table. His Centurions gathered around him: Piet Alferdinck, *Navigator*; Mary-Elizabeth Suzuki, *Gunner*; Ragnar Piripi, *Purser*; Prasert Hayashi, *Boatswain*; Andreea Dalca, *Chief Engineer*; Djamila Sykora, *Dragoon*; Javier Aritza, *Science Officer*.

Council of War.

"I beg your pardon?" Zakhar turned and said to Javier.

Had he been speaking aloud?

He had.

"I said, it's time for a Council of War," Javier finally replied, drawing ugly looks from several others.

Not Sykora, he noted dryly.

"And why is that, Aritza?" Zakhar asked.

"It was a trap," Javier observed in a heavy voice bordering on planet-crushing anger. "Charge me another quarter drachma, but I was right."

The others stirred and muttered under their breath, but didn't say anything.

Zakhar fixed him with that dread captain's stare.

"I'm sure you've always had enemies, Sokolov," Javier continued. "They've either gotten bolder, or more desperate."

He paused to look at everyone at the table that would meet his eye. Andreea might catch him in the reflection from the tabletop, which would be good enough. She was like that.

"Part of that is my fault, I'll grant you," Javier said into the silence. "Navarre did some dangerous and desperate things, and Walvisbaai seems to have made common cause with the asshole who owns the Land Leviathan."

Zakhar's eyes bored into his.

"Why do you care, Javier?" he growled. "You're very close to paying off your debt. You'll be free to go. I made you that promise. I intend to keep it. This won't be your problem shortly."

Javier's stomach turned sour, but the words needed to be said.

"It won't ever stop being my problem, Zakhar," Javier responded. "As long as any of them are alive. Something Del said earlier. Someone might recognize me somewhere, someday. Someone will track you and follow me. I will never escape. Unless I kill all of them."

"All of them?" Sykora asked.

Javier couldn't tell if her voice bordered on mocking, or aroused. It was a fine edge with her.

He fixed her with a death glare.

"All of them," he agreed. "But I've been listening to the damage reports, and you have a problem."

Zakhar didn't say anything, but Javier could see it in his eyes.

"If we were a warship on active duty, I would expect us to need several months in drydock to repair the damage *Ajax* did to us," Javier said.

Zakhar just nodded.

"And we can't afford that," Sykora said, for him. "We're done."

Sykora. Agreeing with Javier.

Had they fallen through Alice's mirror, somewhere along the way?

Yes. At *Shangdu*.

Farouz.

Everyone else in the room disappeared as Javier focused his attention on Zakhar Sokolov, and Djamila Sykora, seated on the man's right. As was normal.

"We are not necessarily done," Javier retorted. "But there are not many options. Especially if you want to get those bastards as badly as I do. Hurt them. Destroy them."

He took a breath. Cast the dice.

"I know a way."

Sykora nodded.

She was in. Just like that.

Crazy and dangerous were her stock in trade.

Zakhar gave him a dose of stinkeye.

Everyone else remained silent, unwilling to fall into the chasm that surrounded the three of them.

"How?" the captain finally asked.

"The derelict is not in any of my records," Javier said. "Partly because it is almost impossible to get to. Partly because of the legend. Partly because I'm greedy and wanted to salvage that derelict myself one of these days, after I was done with survey contracts. I'm pretty sure nobody but me could get us in there, or back again."

He took another breath. Deep. Not cleansing, because it was not clean, mountain air around them.

More like the brimstone fumes one would find in hell.

That was okay. He had escaped all that once. Beat it.

Become somebody else along the way. Someone who was happy.

It wasn't anger drawing him back, pushing him to that spot where he would contemplate doing something like this.

No, this was wrath. Pure and simple.

His eyes locked, first with Sykora, then Sokolov.

She understood and nodded, those bright, green eyes inquisitive, but never doubtful. If the science officer thought he could do it, so could she.

That included storming the Gates of Hell.

The captain studied him more closely. A mad line of electricity connected them across the table.

The *Bryce Connection*.

The rest of Sokolov's Centurions had been minor officers in minor navies. Only he and Zakhar represented the *Concord*. The good guys. The protectors of the galaxy after *Neu Berne* went down in muted flames to end *The Great War*, taking the *Union of Worlds*, *Balustrade*, and almost everyone else down with them.

Only the *Concord* survived.

Hegemon, largely by default.

Wrathful angels coming to take your souls.

"Derelict?" Zakhar asked in a hesitant voice.

As if his soul recognized the danger before his mind did.

"The final resting place of the *Hammerfield*," Javier announced.

Sykora jolted, exactly as if Javier had reached across the table and backhanded her.

"You lie," she snarled.

Javier could understand her pain, her anger.

Hammerfield had an Arthurian quality in *Neu Berne* culture. The last flagship of the *Neu Berne* navy had just disappeared, gone, away to Avalon at the end of the Great War, but it would return in that nation's greatest need.

It hadn't, for reasons known only to the Creator and whatever ghosts had been aboard her.

"You're sure?" Zakhar asked.

Javier nodded.

"Before you," he said with a cold, menacing edge only slightly pointed at this man. "When I could sit patiently at the edge of one of the messiest star systems I had ever seen. Spend weeks, plotting every moon, every asteroid, and every comet to be seen. See the quiet transponder code of the *First Rate Galleon Hammerfield*, Flag of the *Neu Berne* Fleet, before she disappeared from history forever, eighty-five years ago."

"Just like that?" Zakhar said.

Sykora seemed to have gone catatonic. Impressive enough in and of itself.

"No," Javier growled. "It will take a navigation feat for the ages to get close to her. Plus, she was an AI ship, so Creator only knows if the *Sentience* is still alive, let alone sane. If we do get close, the *Sentience* will probably think we're the enemy. *Union of Man*, or maybe *Balustrade*. We'll have to fool it long enough to lobotomize it. Then I'll have to reprogram the AI. Maybe from scratch."

"Is it worth it?" Zakhar asked in an empty voice.

For once, Javier could see all the way into the man's soul. The pain. The strain of holding *Storm Gauntlet* together for more than a decade, in face of all comers. Of doing evil, of *becoming* evil, for what he had told himself were higher goals. See the cost of denying himself a happily-ever-after with Djamila Sykora, when she would have happily walked away with him.

The fear of losing it all. Everything.

For nothing.

"You have dealt honestly with me, Zakhar," Javier said, committing his honor, his own soul, to the task. *The Bryce Connection*. "I want my freedom, not just from you, but from all of them. But I want my revenge, more. *Storm Gauntlet*'s done. You can join me as a partner, or walk away and be done with it. I'll go kill them myself."

Zakhar retreated inside himself for a brief time. Then his eyes started on the captain's left and made their way around the table one by one, making eye contact, before coming to rest on the dragoon.

She nodded. Nothing more.

Tight. Sharp. A blank wall of a face.

It still spoke volumes.

Javier considered the future.

Futures.

All possible tomorrows?

Zakhar turned back to the science officer.

Javier could see tears at the back of those eyes, unspoken.

Zakhar Sokolov made a fist with his left hand, and rapped it down once on the table, a hollow bang as his Academy ring, *Class of '49*, thunked heavily on the hard surface.

The universal greeting among men of the *Concord* Fleet, anywhere in the galaxy.

"Let's go get those bastards."

READ MORE!

Be sure to pick up the other books in The Science Officer series!

The Science Officer
The Mind Field
The Gilded Cage
The Pleasure Dome

You can also get volumes 1-4 collected together in
The Science Officer Omnibus 1

ABOUT THE AUTHOR

Blaze Ward writes science fiction in the Alexandria Station universe: The Jessica Keller Chronicles, The Science Officer series, The Doyle Iwakuma Stories, and others. He also writes about The Collective as well as The Fairchild Stories and Modern Gods superhero myths. You can find out more at his website www.blazeward.com, as well as Facebook, Goodreads, and other places.

Blaze's works are available as ebooks, paper, and audio, and can be found at a variety of online vendors (Kobo, Amazon, iBooks, and others). His newsletter comes out quarterly, and you can also follow his blog on his website. He really enjoys interacting with fans, and looks forward to any and all questions-even ones about his books!

Never miss a release!

If you'd like to be notified of new releases, sign up for my newsletter.

I only send out newsletters once a quarter, will never spam you, or use your email for nefarious purposes. You can also unsubscribe at any time.

http://www.blazeward.com/newsletter/

ABOUT KNOTTED ROAD PRESS

Knotted Road Press fiction specializes in dynamic writing set in mysterious, exotic locations.

Knotted Road Press non-fiction publishes autobiographies, business books, cookbooks, and how-to books with unique voices.

Knotted Road Press creates DRM-free ebooks as well as high-quality print books for readers around the world.

With authors in a variety of genres including literary, poetry, mystery, fantasy, and science fiction, Knotted Road Press has something for everyone.

Knotted Road Press
www.KnottedRoadPress.com

65171778R00082

Made in the USA
San Bernardino, CA
28 December 2017